Driving Lillian

Lockets and Lace Book 17

Sophie Dawson

Lillian desperately wanted to drive a motorcar. Vernon wanted Lillian as well as an undamaged vehicle.

Lillian Miller loved all the new inventions, especially the motorcars. Working at Bavarian Jewelry and Watch Repair Shop, her family's jewelry store, she figured she'd never have a chance. Then she met Dr. Vernon Strasser.

Vernon had recently moved to St. Joseph, Missouri to begin his medical practice. When a lovely young lady rushes in saying she needed a doctor, he follows with more than medicine on his mind.

Will Lillian be able to convince him to teach her to drive? Can Vernon handle the exuberance of the lady he wants to court? What are the men who keep coming into the shop wanting, and will it keep them apart?

CHAPTER ONE

St. Joseph, Missouri
June 1910

Lillian Miller pulled open the door to the Physicians & Surgeons Building and ran in. Her heels clattered on the marble floor as she ran across the lobby. A young man carrying a medical bag was approaching.

"Are you a doctor? I need one quickly," she asked, panic in her voice. She grabbed his hand and pulled him out of the building.

"What's the matter?"

"It's Father. He collapsed. Said his legs wouldn't support him. I don't think he can stand. Will's with him."

A motorcar honked as she pulled him across the street.

"How far?" the doctor asked.

"Just at the other end of the block. Bavarian Jewelry and Watch Repair Shop." Lillian kept going as he asked her questions. "William Miller, he's sixty. I don't know what other medical conditions he has. He's been very tired lately."

"What's your name?" he asked.

What he needed to know that for she hadn't a clue. "Lillian Miller."

When they arrived at the shop, Lillian flew in and around the corner of the counter. She knelt beside her father, taking his hand in hers. Looking at her brother, Will, her eyes asked if anything had changed.

The doctor appeared next to her. "I'm Dr. Strasser. Can you tell me what happened?"

"He was standing at that display case," Will said. "He turned around to come to the workbench and his legs went out from under him. I've made him stay lying here until you came."

Dr. Strasser's focus shifted to Matthew's. "Can you tell me your name?"

"Matthew Miller." The words had a slight slur.

"Very good. That's what your daughter claimed it was. I'm glad she was correct." His small joke brought a slight grin to the right side of Matthew's face. "Look up at me, please."

Lillian saw that there was a droop to his left eyelid.

"Squeeze my hands, please, as tightly as you can."

She watched the rest of Dr. Strasser's examination, biting her lower lip.

"You are exhibiting the symptoms of apoplexy. I think it is mild, but we'll need to do more testing to determine how badly you are affected."

Lillian gasped. "Oh, Father." She took hold of his hand.

"Now, Lillian, don't you fret. I'll be fine." Matthew squeezed her hand reassuringly.

An argument ensued between her father and the doctor on whether he'd go to the hospital.

"Father," Will said. "If the doctor thinks you should be in the hospital, then you should listen to him." He turned. "I'm William Miller. Father and I run this shop together."

"Pleased to meet you, though not under these circumstances. Dr. Vernon Strasser." Vernon held out his hand, and Will shook it.

"Mother needs to be told," Lillian said.

"Yes, but don't call her on the telephone. That will only frighten her. You go fetch her, Will, and bring the buggy," Matthew said. "I'm not sure I can walk home, even riding the electric trolley most of the way." He began to roll over, seemingly intent on getting up. Vernon and Will helped him onto his desk chair.

Will stood looking at his father, then turned to Vernon. "Do you think he can get upstairs to the apartment?"

"Between us, I think we can get him there safely."

Although Matthew was weak, he was able, with Vernon and Will's support, to climb the stairs. They settled him on Lillian's bed while she fluttered around trying to help but also stay out of the way.

Will left to fetch their mother. Dr. Strasser stayed, taking Matthew's pulse and reexamining his abilities.

"I'm going to leave for a while," he said. "I have patients I need to visit. I'll telephone before I come, if I can have your number."

Lillian wrote it on a piece of scratch paper and walked him down the stairs. When she closed the door, she locked it, and placed the Closed sign into view.

As she walked up the stairs, she thought about the young doctor. He was so handsome. Tall with sandy blond hair, combed back away from his face. Already being a doctor, he had to be older than her twenty years. Maybe he graduated early, or he was only beginning his practice. He did seem very capable. He had seemed to appreciate her looks, as she'd caught him eyeing her several times while he was here. Maybe she could invite him to stay for supper if he came back late enough.

~~~~~

Vernon climbed onto the trolley and grabbed a strap to hold on to. He'd finished his house calls and telephoned the jewelry shop. Lillian's sweet voice answered. He knew he should think of her as Miss Miller, but he didn't want to. She'd told him her father was sleeping and that her mother was there.

Lillian's beautiful face seemed to be burned in his mind. Eyes of silver blue that seemed to shout joy even in her worry over her father. Long lashes framed them, making them the highlight of her face. Skin that shone like ripe peaches covered her cheeks. A pert nose over lips the color of terra-cotta that seemed to be formed for kissing.

Vernon thought over the day. He'd known there would be a specific need for his services. Known as soon as he woke up that morning. He'd been right and had known it when Lillian rushed into his office building earlier that afternoon.

She'd seemed so vulnerable. So afraid for her father. Afraid she might lose him. He'd wanted to wrap his arms around her. Give her what comfort he could. He hadn't, of course. That wouldn't have been appropriate, as either a physician or a single man.

Pulling the bell cord, Vernon stepped off the trolley and up the few steps to the jewelry shop. The welcome sight of Lillian opening the door had him grinning like a mad fool. He cleared his throat and pulled his expression to one of serious nature.

"He's still asleep." Lillian locked the door and he followed her up the stairs.

"He'll need to rest. His body has gone through a shock and needs to recuperate," Vernon explained when Mrs. Miller, Lillian, and Will were seated in the parlor. "I'll come by every couple of days to check on his progress. In about a week, he'll have an exercise regimen to do daily. It will help him regain his strength."

Vernon pulled out his pocket watch. "It's late enough in the day, I can stay until he wakes and help him down the stairs." He didn't want to leave. There was a young lady who piqued his interest.

"I'd be most appreciative, Dr. Strasser," Mrs. Miller said. "My sons-in-law are still at work. Having another strong man along with Will to help my husband down the stairs takes a worry off my mind."

Lillian served tea and cookies. He noticed her peeking shyly at him. He smiled and sipped his tea.

Another young woman came up the stairs. Will introduced her as Mrs. Ward, who lived with Lillian in the apartment. Vernon watched as Will explained the situation with

Mr. Miller. He wondered why the woman was living with Lillian.

"Luella." Mr. Miller's call brought them all to their feet. His wife hurried into the bedroom. Vernon followed Will and Lillian.

Lillian, Mrs. Ward, and Vernon stood on the sidewalk after he and Will helped Mr. and Mrs. Miller into the buggy. He knew he should leave, but didn't want to. He wanted to get to know Lillian better.

"Dr. Strasser," Lillian said, a shy note to her voice. "Would you like to stay and have supper with Mrs. Ward and me as a thank you for your quick response to my inquiry for aid?"

Vernon bowed slightly. "No thanks are necessary, but I would be honored to dine with you."

~~~~~

Lillian was nearly bouncing up the stairs. Dr. Strasser was staying for supper. That must mean he was interested in her, right? Or was he interested in Pearl? That thought made her nearly trip on the top step.

No, Pearl was still in mourning for her husband. Besides, she had only just come home from work. She'd barely spoken to the handsome young doctor. No, it had to be herself that he was interested in. She'd seen how he was stealing glances at her, both earlier and after he'd returned from his house calls.

Pearl followed Lillian into the kitchen. "You go entertain Dr. Strasser. I'll make supper. What were you planning?" Her grin told Lillian she knew what her friend was interested in.

Lillian hugged her. "Braised veal cutlets, mashed potatoes, sliced tomatoes, and I made your yeast rolls. There's tapioca pudding for dessert, and fresh butter in the crock."

Shooed into the parlor, Lillian found Dr. Strasser studying the family photograph hanging over the davenport. It had been taken last year in the summer, behind her parents' house.

Dr. Strasser looked so very fit in his linen suit. How had he kept it from being all wrinkled after a day of work? His shoulders were broad. His jacket hugged his torso down to narrow hips. She pulled her eyes back up, hoping she wasn't blushing.

"You have a very handsome family, Miss Miller." Dr. Strasser turned to her.

"Thank you. I'm sure you can tell who my siblings are." The family resemblance was evident in the faces of the three young ladies and one young man.

"Here is Will." Dr. Strasser pointed. "And here you are. Who are these others?"

"This is Mary. She's the oldest. Her husband Clyde Bethel and their children, Anna, Junior, John, and Ruth. Josephine who we call Josey and Fred Gibson, Eddie, and Helen."

"A fine family."

"Are you from St. Jo?" Lillian sat on the davenport and patted the seat hoping he would sit next to her. She looked down, hiding her grin from him.

"No, I grew up in Kansas City, Mo. Not that far from here. And before you continue with the inquiries, my mother is Anna, father, Horace, older sister, Agatha, but we call her Aggie on threat of death, and my younger brother, Nathan. I have an uncle whom I'm named after who is also a doctor which is why I decided to move to St. Jo. He's Dr.

Vernon Strasser too. Didn't want us getting confused by patients."

Lillian wanted to ask more questions about his background, but decided to change the subject. She didn't want him to think he was being questioned by the police. "It's been a lovely spring, hasn't it?"

"Yes, lovely."

When she glanced up at him, he was staring at her and she got the impression he was complimenting her. Heat flushed her cheeks.

"Supper is ready," Pearl said from the doorway to the kitchen. They rose to join her. Lillian's stomach burst into butterflies when he placed his hand on the small of her back, guiding her into the kitchen.

CHAPTER TWO

Lillian was worried. Very worried. Something was wrong with Pearl. She was tired and not as carefree as she had been after moving in with Lillian. By sharing the apartment, Pearl's expenses had dropped significantly. The illness and death of Pearl's husband had left debts and no income.

She'd gotten a job at Townsend and Wyatt Dry Goods Store, but nearly starved before she received her first paycheck. When Pearl had fainted from hunger at the shop when she was selling her watch locket, the Miller family had taken her under their wing, allowing her to sell her Irish crochet lace at their shop. The sales were augmenting Pearl's income allowing her to put away some savings. She'd seemed so happy lately,

17

though she still had times of grief for her late husband.

Recently, however, there was a tension and an almost frantic anxiety to her friend. She was crocheting until her fingers cramped.

~~~~~

Vernon fought a grin as he exited Mr. Miller's bedroom after his thrice weekly house call. Not only was Mrs. Miller waiting to hear his assessment, Lillian was too. After she'd found out, or figured out, when he was coming, Lillian was always at her parents' house.

Once he'd varied the time of day for his visit and the next time he'd received what he could only term the 'evil eye' from her. Now, if there was anything he felt Mr. and Mrs. Miller needed privacy to discuss before others knew, he'd tell only Mr. Miller before speaking to the ladies. Mr. Miller's only comment when Vernon mentioned allowing the couple to decide what and when to tell their children had been, "Lillian's always been a feisty minx."

He'd left his patient knowing Lillian would be angry. Maybe not with him, since it was her parents keeping something from her, but he absolutely knew he'd hear about it. She might even storm into his office to let him have it. Oh well, he could handle it, or her.

"Mr. Miller is progressing well. I've given him permission to go to the shop for an hour or two a couple of times a week. But he's not to push himself too much. We don't want a setback." He watched Mrs. Miller's eyes light up. She'd hurry in to talk with Mr. Miller as soon as Lillian left. Maybe he could talk her into leaving with him. The elder Millers had a bit of planning to do. "I'll also be reducing my visits to once a week."

"Thank you, Dr. Strasser. That's good news. I'll make sure he doesn't overdo." Mrs. Miller smiled. "May I see you out?"

"I do believe I know the way, Mrs. Miller," Vernon said with a smile. "I would be willing to escort your daughter back downtown." Vernon switched his focus to Lillian. "If you are ready to go that is. Mr. Miller said you've been here a while. He seemed to think you were neglecting the shop."

Lillian giggled. "He would whether I'd been here five minutes or five hours. I'll take you up on the offer on one condition; you pay for the trolley." Her eyes twinkled with mischief. She was so pretty. The pale green of her bodice brought out the rosiness of her cheeks.

"Lillian," her mother scolded, "that's so rude. If you need trolley fare, I can give you the coins."

Vernon waved away her protests. "I'm more than willing to foot the bill for the honor of escorting Miss Miller home." He watched her cheeks bloom bright red.

Lillian stammered, "I'll just go say goodbye to Papa." She fled into the bedroom.

"Your husband said she was a feisty minx and I'm seeing he's right." Both he and Mrs. Miller chuckled as Lillian and her father came out into the hall.

~~~~~

Lillian watched Pearl as they fixed supper. Her eyes had dark shadows under them. Her shoulders drooped. Something was definitely wrong, and she intended to find out what it was. She wasn't her mother's daughter for nothing. Determination was practically her middle name.

Only she and Pearl sat down to eat. Will was dining with their parents tonight. It seemed that he stayed late at the shop several times a week, joining them for the evening meal. Lillian knew he didn't like to cook and barely knew how. She also wondered if Pearl was a draw.

Will had rearranged the back part of the shop, even moving the counter and several display cases forward to make more room. He'd brought an old sewing chair from home and set it at the end of the workbench. His end of the workbench. It was for Pearl to sit in when she was there on Saturdays. Lillian could sit in the chair during the week, but it seemed to be reserved for Pearl on the weekend.

"You go on to the parlor. I'll just wipe the table and be in momentarily," Lillian said. As she ran the dishcloth over the table, she watched Pearl walk into the other room, pick up her crocheting, and sit down. Rather than take her work from the bag, Pearl just sat, staring off into space. With determination, Lillian finished her task. She was going to get to the bottom of what was wrong with her friend.

Rather than settling into the sewing chair, Lillian sat next to Pearl on the davenport. Taking her friend's hand, she looked at the pale weary face. "Pearl, what's wrong? No, don't deny it. I can tell something is. You come home from work exhausted. You fall asleep early in the evening, sitting here while we chat and do our handwork. This morning you overslept, nearly to the point of being late for work. I had to wake you up. I'm so worried. Are you ill?"

She watched as tears gathered in Pearl's eyes. Her heart clenched. Pearl had become more than a close friend over the past few weeks. Lillian was beginning to love her like a sister.

She gathered Pearl into her arms. "What is it? Whatever it is, I'll help anyway I can. I know Will would, too."

Pearl drew back. "Oh, you mustn't tell him. No, please."

"Sweetheart, unless I know what's going on I can't promise anything."

Pearl gave a small bitter laugh. "Patrick gave me something before he got sick. It's something we wanted so much. Then he died. Now, I don't know whether to be happy or sad. Thankful or terrified. I bounce between the emotions so many times each day. It's going to be so difficult, but God will provide. He did with you wanting me to live here. Maybe I'll be able to support myself only on the crocheting, but I don't know. There's just so much uncertainty. I'm just so tired all the time, it's hard to think."

"I don't understand. You'll have to be more specific. What is the matter? Are you ill?"

"No, not ill. I'm expecting."

Lillian stared at her friend. Relief followed by joy swamped her. What a blessing. No wonder Pearl was so tired, after working all day on her feet. Then, Lillian realized why Pearl was concerned. "You're afraid you are going to lose your job."

"I'm certain I will lose my job. As soon as it becomes obvious that I'm in the family way, I will be let go. Then, how am I going to support myself and the baby? Even after it is born, I can't be gone all day working. Who will take care of it? Where are we going to live? How will I make enough money making lace to feed, clothe, and afford a place to live?"

Tears slid down Pearl's face. Lillian hugged her again. She didn't know what to say ot how to fix the situation.

"Please, Lillian, please, don't tell anyone. At least not yet. It will come out soon enough. I need time to figure out what I'm going to do. If Mr. Dimmick finds out, I'll be fired. I need the job for as long as I can hold it."

Lillian released the hug and patted Pearl's hand. "I won't say a word. We'll find a solution. You know you can stay here with me for as long as you want."

"Thank you. You're a dear friend, and I love you."

"I love you, too. Now, you have a shawl to finish that will earn you a very good commission, and I have these curtains to hem. Before we get busy with those, we are going to take your situation to the only One who knows how it will end."

The two women joined hands, bowed their heads, and began to pray.

~~~~~

"Drat." Vernon looked at his pocket watch again. He'd knocked it against a table and the cover was dented and the crystal cracked. It wouldn't close, so he needed it repaired immediately. At least it was still running. He was done with his appointments and house calls for the day, so he was leaving the office early. Maybe Will could fix the dent and make it close. He could wait to have the crystal fixed, but he needed the watch for his work.

Vernon locked his office and hurried from the Surgeons and Physicians Office Building. He waved to colleagues rather than stopping to chat.

"What a pleasure to see you again, Dr. Strasser." Lillian smiled at him from behind the counter. "What brings you in such a hurry?"

"I've damaged my watch and it won't close. Would it be possible for Will to look at it, and maybe do a temporary fix so I can use it? I need a watch when I do exams. Counting pulses, getting to my next appointment on time." He held the watch in the palm of his hand. The cover was bent on the edge.

Lillian took the watch and examined it. "You messed it up well. The crystal is broken too."

"I know. That can wait but I really need the watch and to be able to close it."

"How about we loan you a watch so Will can take his time fixing it? We have some we do that with at times." Lillian dug in a drawer under the display case.

"That will be fine. Though it's running, it would probably be a good idea to check the insides to be sure nothing is damaged." Vernon took the watch she held out to him. It was a plain watch with no engraving or decoration on the cover. His watch was more expensive with his initials engraved on the cover amongst intricate designs.

"Dr. Strasser, my brother, myself, and Mrs. Ward are going to the Robidoux hotel for supper tonight. Would you be interested in joining us? To make up a fourth at the table?" Lillian's cheeks bloomed with color as she made the request.

Vernon didn't hesitate in accepting the invitation. Anything to spend more time with the beautiful, animated Miss Miller. "I'd be pleased to join you. Thank you for inviting me."

"Will went home early to change. He will be back here shortly before six o'clock. That will give Pearl and I a chance to change into more appropriate garments for such a grand establishment."

"Then I shall do the same. Thank you for the loan of the watch. I look forward to joining the three of you for supper. Until, later." Vernon smiled, hooked the loaner watch onto his watch chain and left to freshen up for the sudden opportunity to get to know the Millers and Mrs. Ward better.

~~~~~

Since the Robidoux Hotel was only a few blocks from the Bavarian Jewelry and Watch Shop, the two couples walked. Lillian was on Vernon's arm and Pearl was with Will.

"You are looking quite fetching tonight, Miss Miller," Vernon said, looking down. She was wearing a gown of lavender with a darker sleeveless jacket. Steel balls hung along the hem. Large sleeves gathered into long cuffs. Valenciennes lace decorated the cuffs and skirt.

Lillian felt her cheeks heat with his compliment. "Thank you, Dr. Strasser. Have you been in the Robidoux Hotel before?"

"Not past the lobby. I stepped in one day as I walked back to the office. It's very beautiful. The entire room is made of marble in white, gray, and rose. Velvet in a deep rose color is used on all the furnishings. It's very luxurious."

When they arrived, the couples spent some time looking around the lobby. Lillian ran up a short flight of steps and took a drink from the marble fountain on the wall of the landing.

"Must you dash about, Lillian?" Will complained.

"Oh, you sound just like Mother. I didn't do anything wrong." She turned away from him with a swish of her skirts. From the corner of her eye, she saw Dr. Strasser pinch his lips together to keep from grinning. "Let's go on into the dining room. I'm hungry." She took the doctor's arm and towed him along.

Lillian looked around as they were escorted to their table. The high ceiling of the room as well as the walls were of deep green marble with bronze trim. Electric sconces gave off a soft glow from all the columns in the room.

Once they were seated Pearl said, "I've never been in such an elegant place before.

Thank you for bringing me here. It's something I'll always remember."

"It's fitting for our little celebration," Will touched her hand.

Ah, so Will was interested in Pearl as more than just a friend. Maybe something would come of this relationship. It would be nearly a year before he could make his interest in her known. Not until her mourning time was finished. Lillian hoped she could help Pearl until then. She'd do whatever it took to help her and the baby.

"Pearl, um, Mrs. Ward, delivered a commissioned shawl last Saturday and today she accepted a commission for a lace wedding gown." Lillian beamed a smile at Pearl.

"Congratulations, Mrs. Ward," the doctor said. "You must be very pleased."

"Thank you, Dr. Strasser. I am. I never imagined I could make a living doing Irish lace crochet."

The waiter came, poured glasses of wine, and they placed their orders. Once they were alone, Will lifted his glass. "To Pearl being successful in her crocheting endeavors. We are here celebrating another happy event."

"I also have a commission to celebrate. Mr. Norbury is planning a party for his wife's birthday. He didn't tell me how old she will be, but he inferred it was a milestone. To mark the occasion, he has asked me to make a matched set for her. It will be platinum and diamonds. A necklace, bracelet, earrings, and tiara."

"Oh my, Will," Lillian exclaimed. "That's wonderful. Isn't it, Dr. Strasser? My brother is a very talented jeweler. He creates beautiful pieces." She smiled at the doctor, then drew her eyebrows together and looked at Will. "How come I didn't know about this? You didn't tell me."

"You've been visiting father the times he's come in to discuss it. Until it was certain and the deposit made, I didn't want to say anything. That's done, and I've ordered the gems and platinum. I'll begin working on the pieces as soon as they arrive."

"Congratulations, Will," Pearl said, laying her hand on his arm. "I'm delighted for you. We'll both be working on important orders at the same time."

"Yes, we will. I'm going to try and get caught up on all the repairs and smaller orders by the time the metal and gems arrive. I'll be able to concentrate on the set without worrying about my other customers. Plan for me to be staying late most evenings."

"And for us to feed you supper," Lillian teased. Will just grinned at her. Pearl's smile told Lillian, her friend was attracted to her brother. Interesting.

"Do you have the designs planned?" Pearl asked.

"I've been working on them at home in the evenings. They aren't finalized. Mr. Norbury is coming in next week, and we'll work out all the details then."

"Well, this is a celebration, indeed," Dr. Strasser said. "I'd like to mark this auspicious occasion by asking you all to include me within your friendship and call me by my given name, Vernon. I feel sort of left out being called Dr. Strasser when you are more familiar with your address to each other."

A wide smile swept across Lillian's face. "I believe that is a marvelous idea. We can be Vernon, Will, Pearl, and Lillian to each other."

"I have an idea," Vernon said, leaning forward a little with his eagerness. "The Fourth of July is a week from Monday. I hear they are having some special events at Lake Contrary Amusement Park. The four of us could spend the day. What do you say?"

Lillian and Pearl squealed then giggled in delight. An entire day with Vernon. Lillian couldn't wait.

CHAPTER THREE

Lillian sat on the garden swing with her three nieces in the opposite seat. It was Sunday afternoon. The entire Miller family was spending it together. Lunch was over and the little ones would be put down for a nap shortly. They'd begged Aunt Lillian to swing them first. She couldn't deny them. They were so cute.

She loved her family to death, but was wanting to have one of her own. Her own little girls to dress in cute dresses and bows. Boys who would look just like their father.

She closed her eyes at the thought and Vernon's face came before her. Would he be the one for her? She was very attracted to him. Very attracted. He was so sweet, so patient, so good looking. There was one more week before the fourth of July. One more family gathering before the Monday she'd get to spend with him.

Will and Pearl would be there, but they'd be together as a couple. Without saying a thing, Lillian could tell there was something going on between them. She wished there was a way they could get together sooner than next April.

Her thoughts turned back to her being on Vernon's arm for the entire day. They'd made plans at their celebratory supper for how they would spend the day. Since then, Lillian had been searching the papers for every advertisement for the events planned for Lake Contrary Amusement Park. She was sure Will and Pearl were tired of her chattering on and on about it.

"Come, children. It's time for a nap. Aunt Lillian can swing you when you wake up," Lillian's sister Mary called from the back porch.

Lillian helped the little girls down and followed as they ran across the yard. She sat in a wicker chair in the circle the adults had set up in the shade of a huge maple tree. When Mary and Josey came from settling the children, their father stood. It was his method of alerting his offspring that he had something he wanted to say.

"As you can see, I'm recovering well. Thank you all for all you've done for me and your mother. We love you all. In order for me to continue improving, we are going to Hot Springs, Arkansas for the rest of the summer. I'll take the waters there, and your mother will shop. We leave on Friday on the 1:37 pm train."

Shocked gasps and laughter met his statement. Lillian's jaw dropped. She was speechless, a definite first for her. Never had her parents gone out of town without her. Not ever. Doubts flooded through her entire being. Could she function without her parents there to help her if she needed it?

"Are you okay, Lillian?" Her mother stood in front of her.

"I suppose so. Just shocked. You've never been gone before."

Luella Miller sat in a chair next to her, placing a hand on Lillian's arm. "I know you'll do fine. You have your sisters and Will. If you have any problems just go to them. The girls have gone through everything you are and lived through it."

"You're right. It's not like I'm going to be without family to go to." *Not like Pearl*, she thought. She was all alone when her husband died.

Her mother chuckled. "No, Will will be teasing you every day just like always. Besides, I didn't raise you not to be able to handle just about anything." She laughed. "You always took the bull by the horns and wrestled it to the ground. I have no doubt you can handle your parents leaving town for a few weeks."

Lillian thought about what her mother had said. She was right. She was able to deal with whatever might come her way. And if she needed any help, there were more than enough family, and Pearl to help her.

Jumping out of her chair with a bright smile, Lillian grabbed her mother's hand. "Come on, let's go pick out what you want to take with you. If you need anything we can shop for it this week."

They spent the week doing just that. Will complained that Lillian was buying more for herself than helping their mother with all the bags she carried upstairs to the apartment.

They closed the shop for a while on Friday. Everyone but their sisters' husbands were at the train station to see them off. Hugs, tears, and smiles were evident as the older couple saw their trunks loaded and then boarded the train. The children called, "All aboard," echoing the conductor.

As the train pulled out of the station, Will put his arm around Lillian. "We'll be fine. Just think of it as a vacation from mother's intensity."

Lillian chuckled. "I guess so. Poor Will, you only get a vacation from mother. You still have me." The impish grin on her face made him laugh.

"Come on, squirt. We need to get back to the shop." He grabbed her hand and waved to their siblings as they left the station.

CHAPTER FOUR

"Now I'm jealous," Will said as he climbed into Vernon's new automobile. He'd picked his friend up at his house. It was the Fourth of July and they were going to pick up Lillian and Pearl then spend the day at Lake Contrary Amusement Park. Vernon had taken delivery of his new Ford Model T Touring Car. Red with black leather seats, he had the cloth top folded down behind the rear seat.

"Several of the other doctors convinced me to buy an automobile. I'll be able to go on more house calls since I won't have to walk or take the trolley. I can even take patients who live on farms around the area. It should increase my practice." Vernon chuckled.

"Payment, now I'm not so jealous. Let's go get the ladies." Will settled back in his seat as Vernon shifted into drive.

Vernon parked in front of the shop on the side street and turned off the engine. "Do you suppose the ladies will like riding in it?"

"Oh, I know Lillian will. She's been begging Father to buy a motorcar. Pearl, I don't know well enough to say."

They both straightened their linen suits and tapped their straw hats. Will unlocked the shop door and entered.

"Greetings, ladies. You both look lovely, today," Will said. They were dressed in white as was the fashion for the summer months. Wide-brimmed white hats would shade their eyes and faces from the sun. He and Vernon were in off white-linen suits and carried their straw hats while they were in the shop.

"Inferring we do not always look lovely, so it must be noted?" Pearl teased.

Will's face turned bright red with embarrassment.

Stepping past him, Lillian patted Will on the chest. "Don't worry, brother. She's teasing you. Your compliment was lovely in itself. Thank you."

"Yes, Will," Pearl touched his arm. "It was. Thank you."

"So," Vernon began, "are we ready to go to the Park?"

"It will be a while for the trolley to come by." Lillian looked at the large clock on the wall. "Wait. You shouldn't be here yet. The trolley won't be by for another twenty minutes."

Vernon grinned. "We aren't going by trolley. I took delivery of my motorcar this week. It's a touring car so it will hold all four of us."

"You bought a motorcar?" Lillian squealed. "Where is it? Can I drive?" She raced to the door and threw it open, heading out to the street.

Vernon followed her out and found Lillian, hands gripping the steering wheel, bouncing on the seat.

"Crank it on, Vernon," Lillian ordered.

Hands on his hips, he pressed his eyebrows together. "I don't think so, Lillian. It's harder than it looks to drive. I'm still learning myself and don't feel confident to teach you."

"But it must be so much fun, driving so fast down the road. Please, let me drive." Lillian made puppy dog eyes at him.

"No, Lillian, I'm driving."

"Pretty please." More puppy dog eyes.

"I won't be swayed. Just move over so I can start the motorcar. We're wasting the day."

"Oh, all right." She shifted across the leather to the passenger side.

Will cranked and the motor started. Once he was in the back seat next to Pearl, Vernon pulled away from the curb.

"This is so exciting." Lillian was still bouncing. She was also holding on to the door and dashboard, leaning forward on the seat. "I've never been in an automobile before. You absolutely have to teach me to drive, Vernon. I'll never forgive you if you don't. Look how fast we're going. Isn't this great, Pearl?" She kept chattering and waving to those they passed as they traveled the six miles to the amusement park.

Vernon drove onto the grass and stopped. The engine quit, and he turned in his seat so he could look in the rear seat as well as see Lillian too.

"So, what do you think? Did you enjoy the ride?" Vernon asked.

"It was dilly." Lillian was beaming her delight. "When are you going to let me drive?"

"Not any time soon," was Vernon's reply. "Come on. Let's go have some more fun." Vernon jumped out and ran around to assist Lillian down while Will did the same for Pearl.

Lillian hurried them along, eager to get to the midway and the rides. The roof of a ride could be seen rising above the trees. "Oh, look, I can see the Shoot the Chutes ride. I do so want to do that. It's new, just opening this year. Let's do that first." She tugged on Vernon's arm wanting him to move faster.

They walked down the midway, Vernon trying to slow Lillian down. She was so excited, she didn't pay any attention to the attractions and concession stands along the way. She was focused on the lagoon that bisected the midway.

"Look how tall that ride is. I can't wait to try it." She tugged on him again.

When they reached the end of the lagoon, a sled filled with people shot down the incline and into the water. Shrieks and screams followed by laughter filled the air.

"Oh, I so want to do that. Can we go now?" Lillian was fairly jumping in her excitement.

"How about we stroll some more and see what else is here? Look." Will pointed right. "There's the Merry-Go-Round. I heard all the animals have real horse-hair tails."

Vernon noticed a booth and let go of Lillian's arm. "I'll be right back." He went over and the attendant scooped some candy into a bag. Dropping his coins on the counter, he hurried back to their group now standing by the Merry-Go-Round.

He passed a nugget to each, and took one for himself. "I can't believe they had these. They are new, only a couple years old. I've read about them. These candies are taking the country by storm."

"Tootsie Roll." Pearl read the wrapper. "Oh my, that is so good. Chocolate."

Lillian chewed then swallowed the bite she'd taken. "Yummy." She popped the rest of the confection into her mouth. When she'd swallowed, she said, "Let's make sure to buy some to take home before we leave."

"Good idea," Vernon said. "But we may want to purchase them early, as I'm sure they will sell out." He watched her lick her lips. Lips he wanted to taste. Very much wanted to taste.

They walked around looking at the various rides and booths. There was a Figure Eight Roller Coaster and an Old Mill Waterway Ride. Vernon shared a quick look with Will. They'd definitely ride on the Old Mill Waterway Ride. Hopefully, they wouldn't have to share a boat.

"Come on." Lillian tugged on Vernon's arm. "Let's go on the bridge and watch the boats come down the chute. Then, I want to do it. If the rest of you are too chicken to try, I'll go by myself."

Vernon was enjoying her excitement and followed along laughing at her pleasure. When they were standing on the bridge, watching the boats slide down, he stood directly behind her. He wanted to pull her against his chest, nearly reaching out to do so. He stuck his hands in his pockets to keep from doing so.

She might be the one for me, he thought. *It's early days yet. We'll see how not only the day progresses, but how we get along as time passes. The last thing I want is to be tied to someone I don't want to spend time with.*

When another boat started down the incline, Lillian turned, nearly knocking him out of the way in her rush to cross to the other side of the bridge to see it splash into the lagoon. She definitely loved life and seemed to breathe it all in, savoring every moment.

"It does look like fun," Pearl said. "I've never done anything like it before."

"Do you want to get in line now? Or do some of the other rides first? They may seem tame after Shooting the Chutes?" Will asked.

"Oh," Lillian exclaimed. "I hadn't thought of that. Maybe we should do the Merry-Go-Round and the Old Mill Water Way ride first."

"Let's head down that way," Vernon said, placing Lillian's hand on his elbow again. "We can see what else is available to do."

"Look, there's a baseball field. Oh, and they are going to play a game in a couple of hours." Lillian clapped her hands in delight with Vernon's arm between hers.

~~~~~

"We beat you in the race," Vernon laughed.

Lillian swatted his arm. "We were just ahead of them on the ride. It wasn't a race."

Vernon lifted her hand to his lips and kissed the back of it making her fingers tingle. It was the first time he'd demonstrated any affection for her that was other than a friend or brother. "It is if I say so, and I do, and we won."

"I'm hungry," said Will. "Let's go to the fried chicken stand and have some lunch."

"You're always hungry," Lillian teased, "but I'm hungry too." She studied Pearl. She didn't want her friend to become faint from not eating. Pearl was expecting, after all.

"Sounds like a good plan." Vernon tucked Lillian closer to his side as the crowd moved around them.

The men seated the ladies at a table then went to the counter to order their meals. "Are you feeling up to the rest of the day?" Lillian asked, taking Pearl's hand.

"I'm doing well. I'm having such a good time." Pearl's eyes twinkled with merriment. "Vernon seems to be enjoying your company.

Ooooh," she laughed. "You are getting red. You're enjoying his too."

Lillian pressed her hands to her hot cheeks. She was having such a good time. Really, she should be used to getting teased, being the youngest in the family. Being teased about a man's interest was new.

She'd been fairly popular during school, but hadn't been interested in any other boys who wanted to court her. Since then, she worked full-time at the shop. There didn't seem to be any men wanting to court her. Maybe Vernon was interested in her in a romantic way. She certainly was in him.

"Here we are, ladies. Fried chicken, potato salad, and all the rest of the fixings for you to restore yourself for the rest of the afternoon." Vernon set a tray on the table, and Will set out the plates and silverware. He went back for lemonade and soon they were laughing and teasing as they ate the juicy meat with their fingers.

"Let's wait to have dessert," Pearl suggested. "There's an ice cream stand over there." She pointed.

"Good idea. We can have that after the baseball game," Lillian said.

"Do you ladies really want to go to the ball game?" Vernon asked.

"Sure we do, or at least I do." Lillian looked at Pearl. "Do you want to or are you tired." When Will gave Pearl a sharp look, Lillian knew she'd misspoken. Pearl didn't want him to know of her condition. Sure it would become known in time, but it wasn't her news to tell.

"I want to see the game. Who's playing?"

Vernon and Will chuckled.

"A couple of teams from the local league. It's definitely not the major league." Will began gathering up the dirty dishes to return to the kitchen. "How about you ladies go and refresh yourselves. We'll meet you just outside the building."

"I'm so sorry, Pearl." Lillian clasped her friend's hand as they entered the building with the lady's retiring room on one side and the men's on the other. "I shouldn't have asked if you were tired like that. I hope Will didn't notice."

"He looked at me, but I think I covered it well enough. He'll find out soon enough." Pearl hugged Lillian offering comfort for the guilt she had.

"But I don't want to let anything slip. I'm terrible at keeping secrets. My mouth just runs on without my brain being able to catch up."

"Don't worry." Pearl smiled at her. "I'll be sure to cheer enthusiastically during the game. That should assuage any thoughts he might have. I am feeling quite refreshed after our meal."

"It was good, wasn't it? Your idea of having ice cream later is a good one. Come on. Let's get finished in here and find the men. I'll bet Will buys some peanuts. He always wants them when he goes to a game."

~~~~~

"I'm going to get some peanuts," Will said once they'd found their seats in the shade of the grandstand.

Lillian and Pearl burst out laughing.

"What?" he quizzed.

"Lillian said you'd buy peanuts to eat, even though we just finished our lunch." Pearl patted his hand. "You go right ahead. I'm sure we'll eat some too."

Vernon wondered about the relationship between the couple. Was it leading to something? It couldn't progress to anything more than friendship for at least another eight months, at least. That was when her year of mourning would be over. He could tell Will was very attracted to the young widow. Pearl seemed to be interested in Will also.

He glanced across Lillian to study Pearl. She'd been rather peaked before they ate, but now seemed to be recovered. Maybe she just wasn't used to being out in the sun so much. Lillian hadn't seemed affected by the sun and heat of the day. But he didn't think much of anything would dim her enthusiasm.

Will returned just as the first pitch was thrown. Vernon was pleased to see Pearl cheer just as heartily as Lillian was.

"Cracker Jack. Get your Cracker Jack right here." A couple of youths were holding up boxes of the sweet popcorn as they milled through the spectators.

"Oh, Vernon." Lillian grabbed his arm. "Get some, please." Her eyes were wide and pleading as she looked up at him. "We can't be at a baseball game without having some."

"We can't, can we?" Vernon laughed and raised his hand to signal one of the boys. He needed the distraction. He wanted to lean down and kiss those ruby lips as they pursed with her desire. He knew it was for the sweet, but he had the feeling her lips would taste just as good.

Sharing the box with her, Vernon found himself watching her instead of the game. It was a well fought game. Each side making hits and runs, keeping the score close. Lillian and Pearl cheered for both teams. When one of the batters hit a home run, Lillian jumped up, yelling and clapping her hands, nearly knocking the Cracker Jack box from his hand.

At the middle of the seventh inning, a man ran out onto the field and led the crowd in Take Me Out to The Ball Game. Vernon and Will stood and waved their boxes and the bag of peanuts around showing they'd obeyed the directions in the song.

~~~~~

When the game ended, they walked back to the midway. Vernon kept Lillian's hand on his elbow. He'd seen several other men looking at both she and Pearl. He didn't want anyone to think she was available.

"Let's either get ice cream or ride those rides," Lillian pointed to the building where ice cream was sold, then to the Shoot the Chutes and the roller coaster. "The lines aren't getting any shorter."

"How about you ladies get in line and we'll get the ice cream. We can eat it while we wait to ride," Will suggested.

Vernon didn't want to leave the ladies to themselves, but Lillian was already saying they were going to the retiring room then would stand in line for the roller coaster. As they walked away, he asked, "Should we leave them alone? I don't want anything to happen to them."

"Don't worry. Lillian can protect them both. She is her mother's daughter after all. Her tongue can slice a man to ribbons with just a few words." Will turned. "The line's not very long at the ice cream stand. The sooner we get in line the shorter amount of time we'll be away from the ladies."

They rejoined the ladies with paper bowls filled with chocolate ice cream as Lillian and Pearl had requested. It had been cranked earlier and packed in ice to help it harden before being served. They used little wooden paddles shaped like spoons to eat the treat.

"I can't wait to ride this," Lillian said and took another bite of her ice cream. She swallowed and continued, "Have you seen how fast the cars go. I've never ridden a roller coaster before. It's going to be so much fun." She jumped a little, nearly spilling her ice cream.

Vernon chuckled and tipped her bowl so it was level. "Be careful. That chocolate won't look good on your white dress."

"Oh, no it wouldn't, thank you. We saw a little boy with it all down the front of his white shirt. I doubt his mother will be very happy, trying to get the stain out."

They finished their ice cream and Will disposed of the bowls and spoons in a trash barrel. Soon they were next in line to ride the coaster.

"Let's get in the first car, Vernon. I want to see from there."

"You sure you want that? I hear it's the scariest position."

"Yes, I'm sure. I want to be in front." She bounced a little on her toes demonstrating her excitement.

"It's a good thing we're at the front of the line then."

The attendant signaled them forward and they climbed in. Vernon glanced back and saw that Will had reached around Pearl holding onto the bar on her other side. She had a look on her face that told him she wasn't as enthusiastic as Lillian was.

"Do you want my arm around you to secure you?" he asked, knowing the answer before she spoke.

"No, I want to feel the whole thing."

The car began moving, clacking as the chain pulled it up the incline. Lillian looked up at him and smiled. She looked like she was having the time of her life.

Over the top, and then the car flew down, around, up, down, around, jerking them from side to side. Lillian was screaming in delight. On one curve she glanced at him, her smile wide, her eyes alight with joy.

When they stopped back where they'd started, Lillian jumped out. "Wasn't it wonderful?" she asked, and grabbed Pearl's hand. Vernon didn't think Pearl had enjoyed the ride as much as her friend had. "That was so much fun. I want to do it again, but I want to Shoot the Chutes first. Then, we can come back and get in line again. Come on. Let's hurry to get in line."

She grabbed Vernon's hand and dragged him toward the people waiting to Shoot the Chute. When they reached the end of the line, Lillian brought up a topic he'd hoped she'd forgotten.

"When are you going to teach me to drive your car?"

"I'm not going to teach you. It's a brand new car and I need it for my work. It's not a toy."

"I know that. I won't wreck it. Please at least let me drive part way home." Lillian gripped his arm, her eyes pleading.

Vernon knew she'd gotten her way often using those eyes. This time it wasn't going to work. "Absolutely not. Aside from the fact that it will be dark and many people on the road, I'm not going to teach you to drive."

"You're an old stick in the mud," Lillian complained.

"Better me stuck in the mud than my brand new motorcar." Vernon turned from facing her to watching the sled splash into the lagoon.

"Humph." Lillian crossed her arms in front of her.

Vernon kept himself from laughing at her. She wouldn't take his reaction to her pouting well at all.

When it was their turn, the two couples sat next to each other on the seat. The boat was pushed over the edge. A shriek came from Pearl and Lillian laughed the entire way down.

As they climbed out. Pearl's excitement was evident. "Let's go again. That was so much fun."

"Yes, let's do. I loved it." Lillian laughed.

They got back in line and rode it again. Pearl wanted to ride the Chutes again. Lillian wanted to ride the roller coaster. The couples split up, Will and Pearl riding the Chute and Vernon and Lillian alternating between that and the roller coaster.

~~~~~

They were sitting in the shade of the old oak trees, having a drink to revive them after all the rides. The afternoon was waning. They had reservations at the Lotus Club further along the lake for supper.

"We have a ride we haven't tried yet," Lillian said just before she took a sip of the Coca-Cola Vernon had bought her. "Although after the roller coaster and the Chute, it might seem tame."

"What ride?" Will asked.

"The Old Mill Waterway." Lillian pointed. "It looks to be inside and might be cool and refreshing after all this time in the sun. Although you have found a nice shady spot. Besides, the line isn't long like at the other rides. What do you say?"

"I'm for it," Vernon said. "It will be a more relaxing ride than the ones we've been riding. Then we can go to the automobile and drive to the restaurant. That way we don't have to walk back in the dark once the fireworks are over."

Once they'd finished their drinks, they returned the bottles and went to the Old Mill Waterway. Lillian was surprised that the building was dimly lit. She was again when the attendant put Will and Pearl in one small boat and she and Vernon in another. There were larger boats with more seats. They could have shared one. Then Vernon's arm came around her shoulders along the back of the seat.

Before she had a chance to say anything, the attendant pushed them toward the dark tunnel. When she realized that the ride enabled couples a little bit of privacy in the dimness, Lillian kept her mouth shut and snuggled a little closer to Vernon.

Around them was an artificial garden. Artificial trees with stuffed birds were surrounded with flowers in bright colors. Light filtered in, adding to the romantic atmosphere.

Vernon's hand tipped her face toward his. Lillian watched his head descend and his lips approach hers. Then they touched and held.

He tasted of the root beer he'd had. His lips were gentle. Soft against hers. They left hers and she felt bereft. Again his lips met hers, this time more firmly. When he pulled back, Lillian was captured in his gaze.

"Please don't be angry with me, Lillian. I've been wanting to do that all day."

"I'm not, but…" she bit her bottom lip. "What does it mean?"

"It means I want to explore the attraction between us. I'm not promising anything. I'm not making a declaration. But, I want to get to know you better. Court you. See if we are meant to be together. Do you want that?"

Lillian didn't know what to say. Well, yes she did, but she needed to still her racing heart or she'd yell her answer and upset Vernon, Pearl, and especially her brother. She took a deep breath. "Yes, Vernon. I'd like that."

He kissed her again, a short, sweet one. Then they were nearly at the end of the tunnel.

"When you come courting, will you teach me to drive?"

CHAPTER FIVE

Lillian flopped down on her bed. It was a little over a week after the Fourth of July. She'd just failed to keep her promise to Pearl. Will had tricked her. Asked her about Pearl's health, her tiredness as they ate their lunch. It had started simply enough. Then he'd figured it out. He'd asked how far along Pearl was, and Lillian had just told him without thinking. Pearl was going to hate her.

At least Will had promised not to say anything. Not reveal that he knew Pearl was expecting. He was trying to figure out how they could continue to help Pearl. Lillian was too.

She'd let her live with her in the apartment above the shop for free if Pearl would let her. Lillian loved to sew. If Pearl used her employee discount to purchase fabrics and thread, Lillian could help by sewing the layette. That would help. But Lillian knew that however she helped, it wouldn't be enough. Well, Lillian would do as much as she could to ease the burden, supporting her friend in whatever way she could.

Glancing at the clock, Lillian sat up. She needed to go downstairs and tend the shop while Will worked on the commission pieces. They were coming along and were beautiful. She was so proud of her brother. He was more talented than either their father or grandfather. This commission could change his life, bring him more commissions, and set him up as a jeweler in his own right rather than mostly a watch repairman.

She rose and wiped her face with a damp cloth. My, it was hot. Mid July was always hot and humid. Well, at least it would be cooler this evening. Vernon was coming to visit when he was finished with his patients for the day. Now, if she could just keep her big mouth shut so she didn't spill the beans about Pearl to him.

~~~~~

Vernon parked his car beside the jewelry shop. He was going to take Lillian out to supper, then dancing. At least, he hoped it would be dancing. He knew Lillian wanted to go to the movie house and see what was playing. He supposed they could do both. The movie wouldn't be all that long.

He was just getting out of the car when Lillian came out of the shop, ready to go. She was smiling. At least her mood was better than a couple of weeks ago. She'd been so pensive for a few days, he'd begun to worry that her interest in him as a beau was waning.

"Hi, Vernon, I'm all ready to go. Where do you want to eat tonight? I heard about a new diner on the south side of town. I hear they serve hot dogs and Campbell's Pork & Beans. I thought that sounded good. I think they have hot fudge sundaes too. What do you think? I have the address right here." She dug into her purse. "Well, it's here somewhere. Just head south. I'll find it before we get too close."

Vernon smiled as he helped her into the passenger seat. She was still chattering about hot dogs and beans. Seems they were going to have that for supper. As he got behind the wheel, she held up the paper.

"Found it." She told him the address and pointed in the direction she wanted to go. "We heard from Father and Mother today. We got a long letter. They are doing well in Arkansas. I miss them, but they seem to be having a good time. Father can walk three miles now. He says his strength is getting better every day. Isn't that wonderful?"

She went on chattering, and he listened to the excitement and happiness in her voice. Seems she'd gotten over her melancholy.

"You certainly are quiet tonight, Vernon. Do you feel okay?"

He laughed. If he'd been stopped he'd have leaned over and kissed her, but he was driving so he just glanced at her and laughed. "Just when have I been able to get a word in edgewise?"

"Oh, have I been chattering? It's a bad habit of mine. Will complains about it all the time. Well, I guess not as much since he bought his house and moved out of the apartment. Pearl doesn't complain. I think she likes my filling the silence. At least, she's never told me to be quiet.

"Oh, there's the diner. Do you see a place to park? Oh, there's one right over there. Hopefully, the horses won't drop things on your motorcar."

When Vernon shifted into park, he looked around, leaned over, and gave her a quick kiss. "Enough chatter. What are you so excited about?"

She seemed to ponder the question. "You came earlier than I expected. I saw you pass the window and turn the corner. I was ready and glad to see you. We'll have more time together before I need to be home." The smile on her face warmed his heart.

"Let's go get some of these hot dogs and beans you are so eager to eat." He came around the vehicle to help her out.

"Don't forget the hot fudge sundaes," she said as she placed her hand in his.

~~~~~

Lillian stared, struck totally dumb by what Will and Pearl had told her. Will had found a way to help Pearl. They were going to get married. Relief and joy bubbled up, needing to be released. She exploded with squeals and hugs, first for Pearl, then Will, then back to Pearl.

Her excitement came to sudden stop. "Have you told anyone else? Have you called Father and Mother? Are you going to? When is the wedding? Am I invited? Can I be the maid of honor? Have you told Mary and Josey? Oh, they will be so excited. Can I tell them if you haven't? They always know everything before I do."

She kept asking questions, not allowing any to be answered until Will finally placed his hand over her mouth.

"We've decided to have a small private wedding. I'm sure you understand, given the circumstances."

"But what about the rest of the family?"

"We'll tell them all at Mary and Clyde's tomorrow after church. After everyone has eaten. It's always better to share something surprising when stomachs are full." Will gave his sister an intense stare. "Don't mention anything to anyone. I'll decide when to announce it. And, don't, I repeat, don't write to Mother and Father about this. It's our news to tell, not yours."

Lillian pursed her lips to the side. "Oh, all right. Mums the word." Suddenly, she grinned. "Can I still be the maid of honor?"

~~~~~

"So, that's the long and short of it. Will and Pearl got married yesterday. The whole family, except Mother and Father, were there. I think Mary and Josey were shocked but are okay with it now. I think that they would have been married next year anyway, after her mourning year was up. All this does is move the timeline up." Lillian stopped talking.

Vernon waited, just in case she started up again. "I think you're right. I noticed his interest in her was intense on the Fourth of July. I also wondered about Pearl's health. She seemed fragile. She hid it well, but I wondered. I'm glad she's not ill."

"Me too." Lillian leaned back against the park bench. They were in the park not far from the shop. Vernon had come by just after the shop closed. Lillian had been somber, but then brightened and told him of the wedding that had occurred the previous day. "Now, I'm living alone in the apartment. Last night was the first time I've ever done that. It didn't really occur to me that Pearl would move out when she and Will married. Stupid of me, huh?"

Vernon gave her hand a squeeze. He hoped she wasn't hinting that he propose. It might come in the future, but he wasn't ready yet. "Are you afraid to stay alone? I'm sure one of your sisters would let you stay with them until your parents get back. Then you could move back there."

Lillian pulled back from leaning on his shoulder. "Are you joking? I'm not planning on moving home. Mother and I were fighting so much, I packed up my bags and moved in with Will without even asking him. It was awful. She was treating me like a little girl, not the woman I am. I'm not twelve anymore. I'm a grown capable woman." She'd straightened her spine as she spoke. "Maybe I'll just become a suffragette and start marching for women to be able to vote." Then she sagged against him. "Even if I do get to vote, I'll still be alone in my apartment."

Vernon stood, pulling her up with him. "Well, you aren't alone right now. I say we head over to the bandshell in Krug Park. There's a concert tonight."

Lillian's eyes lit up. "That's a great idea. Can I drive?" She batted her eyes at him.

"No."

"Party pooper." She grabbed his hand and pulled him toward the entrance to the park.

CHAPTER SIX

"This is going to be so much fun. It's been so hot lately. Canoeing on the lake will surely be cooler than being stuck in town in the shop. I'm so glad you invited me." The day was hot, sunny, with little breeze. A typical Missouri day in early September.

Vernon glanced at Lillian, her usual enthusiasm evident in her slight bouncing on the seat of the motorcar. She'd asked to drive, again, and he'd told her no, again. He was considering teaching her, but wasn't going to mention it. He'd never hear the end of it if he told her that he might. Not that she didn't ask every time they were together anyway.

There was an unease within him. Nothing major, but he felt as if the day wouldn't go as planned. He hoped that he was wrong, but he'd watch out just in case.

Lillian was so cute. He thought her beautiful, most of the time, but today, she was cute. He'd warned her to wear old clothing. One never knew what happened in a boat, and Lillian was always at risk of disaster with her exuberance. She had on a straw hat that had obviously seen better days. The brim was ragged. It had obviously been crushed at some time. Her white blouse, also, was one he hadn't seen before. The cuffs were frayed and it was just a wee bit tight. Maybe left from her school days. Her skirt was a light blue with navy braid along the bottom.

"I'm glad you like the idea. You aren't wishing today wasn't Sunday and you were at Mary's with the rest of the family, are you?"

"Not one bit. I love my family, but being able to spend the afternoon with you is…"

Vernon glanced at her and saw a blush color her cheeks even with the sheer scarf she had covered her face with to keep the road dust off. "Is what?" He grinned, putting his eyes back on the road.

"Special," she finally said.

Vernon parked on the lawn near the boat dock of Lake Contrary. It was about the same spot they'd watched the fireworks from on the Fourth of July. There were several boats and canoes on the water. Families had spread blankets on the ground with picnic baskets. Children and adults played in the shallow water by the beach.

"It's special for me too, Lillian. Every time I'm with you is special." Vernon gazed into her eyes, wishing they were in a more private place. He wanted to kiss her. Maybe they'd boat into the shade of a weeping willow tree, allowing the branches to hide them so he could steal a kiss.

With Pearl not living with Lillian, there weren't the opportunities for him to be in the apartment with her. He wasn't going to ruin her reputation, and she would never allow it.

As one of the younger doctors, Vernon was on call more on Saturdays and Sundays than more established ones. That meant he had to be available for the hospital to call him if he was needed. That limited when and where they could go on those weekend days. This was the first Sunday he'd been able to be available to take Lillian somewhere rather than spend the afternoon at one of her sister's houses with the rest of the family.

Lillian had invited him several Sundays to join the family at Mary and Clyde's home where the entire family was gathering with Mr. and Mrs. Miller still away. Vernon had mentioned to Mary that it might be best if their parents didn't host each Sunday afternoon when they got home. She had agreed and promised to speak with Josey about sharing the days.

"Come on. Quit your wool gathering. Let's go rent a canoe. That's what we came here for, isn't it?" Lillian had unwrapped the scarf and set it on the seat. "I didn't wear this old skirt for nothing. I wish I'd thought to bring my bathing suit. Wouldn't it be fun to go swimming? We'll have to do that next time."

Vernon wasn't sure he'd be able to handle seeing her in one of the new style bathing suits. They were little more than a chemise and drawers, though made of heavier, darker fabrics. Gone were the days of knee-length dresses, heavy socks and swim shoes. He could see several women playing in the water in the garments. Seeing Lillian in one might be too much for him. When wet they showed more of the figure and legs clear up to the thigh. No, he thought it might be best if he waited to see more of Lillian's after they wed.

Vernon stumbled on his way around the vehicle. He hadn't decided on marrying Lillian, had he? Or had he? Did he love her, or was he just attracted to her love of life and sense of adventure? Seeing her opening the door, he hurried to help her descend. He'd have to think on this later. Right now, he was going to enjoy the day with her. Besides, if he was going to propose, he had to wait until her parents came home.

~~~~~

The canoe wobbled when Lillian stepped down into it. She'd never been in one before. Any time her family had boated on the lake, they'd rented johnboats. She sat down quickly on the small seat in the bow. The boatman handed her a paddle once Vernon was in his place at the stern.

"You need to turn around, Lillian. We'll be paddling against each other if we are facing the opposite direction." Vernon grinned at her.

"Maybe I don't want to paddle. If I turn around I won't be able to see you."

"That's true, but I don't think it's fair that I have to do all the work. You are perfectly capable of sharing the load." Vernon gave her a toothy smile.

"Oh all right. You sound just like Will." She could hear him chuckle as she squirmed around on the narrow seat, nearly dropping her paddle. "I'm not sure I'm very good at this. I haven't ever rowed a boat before," she grumbled.

"It's not rowing, it's paddling." She could hear the laughter in his voice.

Lillian loved his laugh. It was hearty and honest. She could tell when someone was faking a laugh. They either laughed too hard at something not that funny, or too little indicating they didn't understand. Or they laughed at you, not with you. Lillian hated that. She'd been laughed at too many times as a child. The product of having too many older siblings.

But, Vernon's laugh just warmed her in her middle. Even when she did or said something that could be laughed at, his was just enough showing he saw the humor, not that he thought she was stupid or dumb for having done or said it.

When she was settled, facing away from him, Lillian lifted her arm and pointed forward. "Cast off, ye landlubber. We've an exploration ta do." Vernon laughed and pushed them away from the dock.

Lillian didn't have a clue as to how to paddle. They were going in circles with Vernon yelling instructions to her that she didn't understand. That he was laughing made it all okay. At least he wasn't getting angry at her ineptitude. She heard some people on the shore and in the water laughing too. She tried to stand and take a bow, but the canoe wobbled, and Vernon yelled for her to sit down. She did. The last thing she wanted was to fall into the water.

"How about you let me paddle? You can just enjoy the ride?" Vernon called to her. "Just lay your paddle on the bottom."

"Oh, good. I don't think I'm made to be a paddler." Lillian squirmed back around so she could see him and set the paddle down. "This view is better anyway." She gave him a cheeky grin.

A look Lillian recognized entered his eyes. "This view is better as well."

Now that Vernon was in control of the canoe, they moved smoothly across the water. The breeze cooled the back of Lillian's neck as she looked around. There were people fishing on the far shore, away from the noise of so many people. Boys were skipping rocks across the calm water. Couples walked along, many with children running beside them.

That was what Lillian wanted; family. She was hoping that would be with Vernon. Since they'd spent the day together the Fourth of July, they'd seen each other most weekends and sometimes during the week. He'd stopped in the shop a couple of times, especially if he couldn't take her out on the weekend. Will teased her fiercely whenever that happened after Vernon left. Once she'd had to escape upstairs because of it since she didn't want for him to see her cry at his teasing. Will had apologized and stopped after that.

The kisses they'd shared in the Old Mill Waterway weren't the only ones he'd given her. Each time they went out, he'd kiss her, sometimes quite passionately. He never mentioned anything about the future though. Was he playing with her affections? Lillian desperately hoped not.

They'd reached the end of the lake and Vernon turned the canoe around. There were weeping willow trees all along the shoreline, hanging out over the water. He guided the craft into the shadows, allowing the branches to enclose them.

The sunshine peeking through the leaves dappled his face. Lillian wished they were back in the Old Mill Waterway ride at the amusement park. She had been so close to him then. He'd first kissed her there. She was all the way at the other end of the canoe. With it being so tipsy, there was no way they could steal any kisses here.

"Maybe we should have taken a johnboat instead of a canoe," Vernon said, his eyes intent on her lips.

"No maybe about it." Lillian licked her lips.

The canoe stopped as Vernon held the paddle across his knees. They sat staring at each other.

A rock hit something above them, thrown by a boy on the shore. It plunked next to the canoe. Vernon's eyes widened, his mouth open in horror. Lillian turned to see, then jumped up, trying to get to him as she saw a hornet's nest drop into the water just ahead of the canoe. The canoe jerked with her movement. Vernon reached for her. An angry buzzing rose behind her. As the canoe tipped, Lillian gave a scream that was cut off as she landed in the water.

~~~~~

Vernon felt the water rise around his head as he flew into the water. He had to get to Lillian. She'd leaped at him as the hornets were flying up at her in an angry swarm. Not only could she drown, but she could also be stung by any number of the insects.

He kicked up and toward where she would have fallen in. A foot hit him in the face. He grabbed it, pulling it to him. He was kicked again, this time in the chest. She was flailing around. He could hear her screams muted by the water. He latched on to her skirt, then wrapped his arms around her legs and pulled her down. Her scream abruptly stopped as her head went underwater.

Vernon let go of her legs and grabbed her around the waist. He kicked up and their heads broke the surface. "Big breath. We're going under again."

For once she didn't say anything, just did as she was told. Hornets were swarming around their heads. He pulled them back under and kicked away from the shore, out from behind the willow branches. He hoped the hornets would stay within the enclosure of the tree.

Surfacing again, he looked around, searching for any hornets still coming after them. His hope was realized as he didn't see any, though he could hear their anger coming from the tree.

"Are you all right?" He examined Lillian's face. She'd been much closer to the nest when it fell. There were several welts rising on her forehead and cheeks. He saw a hornet trying to escape from her wet hair. He knocked it into the water. At least she wasn't struggling against him anymore.

"I have some stings. I lost my shoes. Are you okay? I didn't kick you hard, did I?" Lillian let go of him and began treading water, though he could tell her clothing was weighing her down. They needed to get to shore before she weakened and drowned.

"Hey!" A male voice called from behind him. Vernon turned. Two men in a johnboat were rowing toward them. "We're coming. Are you hurt?"

Vernon began kicking again, this time toward the men in the boat. He realized Lillian was kicking too. "You know how to swim?"

"Yes, my Father taught us all. He had a friend drown when he was a child. Wanted us all to know how." She was panting a little as she spoke.

When the boat was stopped beside them, the men reached down and pulled Lillian from the water, with him pushing on her rear end. She flopped into the boat and the side nearly dipped into the water.

"Lie on the floor, there," one man told her. "Come on. We'll keep the boat steady while you get in."

Vernon took hold of the side and pulled himself up and into the boat with the other man's help. He lay panting on the bottom.

"What happened? We were fishing and heard the commotion?" The man was wrapping a blanket around Lillian's shoulders.

Vernon told them of the hornet's nest and their escape from being badly stung.

"We'll get you back to shore. Those men," he pointed, "have got your canoe. They'll get it back to the boatmen."

Vernon sat up and drew Lillian into his arms. "Not quite the way I wanted the day to go."

"Me neither." Then she whispered in his ear. "It was romantic for a little while there though."

Leave it to Lillian to see the positive in a negative situation.

CHAPTER SEVEN

"Please, no, Mary," Lillian complained. "I'll look awful, all spotted if you put calamine on the stings." Mary didn't care as she continued dabbing the pinkish-tan liquid on Lillian's face.

Once the men had taken them to shore, Vernon and she had gone to the motorcar. He'd dug a couple of blankets out of his trunk, and laid them over the seat, not wanting to soak the leather.

Lillian hadn't wanted to come to her sister's, but he'd insisted. She needed dry clothing and tender care after their ordeal, he'd said. She didn't want her family to know what happened, even though it hadn't been her fault. At least this time.

Her nieces and nephews were playing in the front yard when they arrived and alerted their parents to their bedraggled state. Mary and Josey had hustled Lillian into the house and up to the bathroom. As they climbed the stairs she heard Will asking what happened and Clyde, Mary's husband, offer Vernon dry clothes.

Lillian now sat, wrapped in Mary's bathrobe, on the vanity chair in Mary's room. She'd had a bath with both her sisters in attendance, coddling her like a toddler. Josey was braiding her hair while Mary covered her face with spots of lotion.

"This will keep them from itching quite so badly. Now, sit still." Her tone was exactly that of their mother.

"At least, as hot as it is, you won't catch a chill," Josey said. "You don't want to miss greeting Mother and Father when they arrive home."

"What? They're coming home?" Lillian turned on the chair to look at Josey.

Mary turned her back to face her. "Yes, I received a letter yesterday. They will arrive on Thursday on the afternoon train." Mary placed one last spot of medicine, then capped the bottle. "We all plan to meet them. You can close the shop for the half hour or so to meet them at the station. Then we'll take them home for a rest. We're going to have a family supper here that evening."

"We're hoping that having the family around will offset some of the shock of finding out about Will and Pearl's marriage." Josey fastened a ribbon around the end of Lillian's braid.

Mary stood. "We'll help you get dressed. I'm sure that young man of yours is wanting to be sure you are truly okay." Mary took Lillian's hand. "He's a good man, Lill. You be sure to keep him."

"I'll try."

They helped her dress in some of Mary's clothes, which were somewhat big on her and too long. They would work until she got home. Other than Lillian's underthings, she'd decided to discard her blouse and skirt. They were smeared with mud and grass-stained since she'd slipped going up the rise to the motorcar and slid down in her wet skirt. Mary was going to wash the rest. Lillian just hoped her corset wasn't ruined.

The children surrounded Lillian when she went downstairs. They wanted to hear all about the adventure of being chased by angry hornets. Clyde insisted they stay for supper. Pearl took Lillian aside and asked if she was truly all right. She reassured her new sister-in-law that she was fine, more embarrassed by the spots on her face than everything else.

Finally, once they'd eaten and the good-bye hugs and kisses from each child were given and received, she allowed Vernon to help her into the passenger seat of his automobile.

"What an afternoon," she said as he climbed in after cranking the motor.

"Not at all what we planned, but I had fun. I always do when I'm with you." He pulled away from the curb on their way to the shop and her apartment.

Lillian leaned her head back and looked at him. Mary was right. Dr. Vernon Strasser was a good man. He'd done everything he could to save her after they fell out of the canoe. He hadn't laughed at her spotted face as Will had done until Pearl batted him on the arm to get him to stop.

They traveled in a comfortable silence, at least for her, until he parked beside the shop. Vernon turned and studied her.

"You'd tell me if you were hurt or felt poorly after our dunking in the lake, wouldn't you?"

His worried expression touched her heart. "Yes, Vernon, I would. I'm fine. You don't think a little water would hurt Lillian Miller, do you? I'm made of stiffer stuff than this." She reached out and touched his cheek. "Despite it all, I had a wonderful time with you. Thank you for inviting me."

Vernon looked around. "There's no one on the street." He leaned over and kissed her softly. "There's no one I'd want to get dumped out of a canoe with more than you."

~~~~~

Vernon hung his sodden suit on the edge of the bathtub. It would have to go to the dry cleaners. His other garments could be washed, though his shoes would have to dry out themselves. He'd bathed and was ready for bed. He gave a sigh as he went into his bedroom. Now, he knew what the feeling was he'd had portended.

He'd only had a few Callings in his life. He didn't seem to have the strong Callings his grandmother Aggie Cutler or his great uncle Nugget Nate Ryder had, and he was always leery of believing in them. They were so few and far between he'd forget what they felt like. It always took him by surprise and a long time to recognize he was having one.

His first had been when he was fifteen and his father had been caught out in a violent storm. Vernon had known his father was in danger. He'd nearly gone mad waiting for the storm to pass so he could go out and search for him.

His mother had had the same Calling. Hers had been stronger. She'd known right where her husband was. She'd taken him straight to the collapsed building he'd taken shelter in. A tornado had gone through the area. They'd found him trapped under a beam. If they hadn't found him, he could have died.

Vernon lay down on his bed and put his arms under his head. He didn't know whether he liked the Callings or not. It wasn't as if he could stop something from happening. Today was witness to that. But then again. Maybe he was ignoring them. Maybe he needed to try to identify them better.

That day he'd met Lillian was a good example of that. There was no reason for him to be in the lobby right then. He had planned to go to his house calls later, and finish some paperwork first. Somehow he had found himself carrying his medical bag and descending the stairs. It was just something he'd had to do. Then Lillian had run up to him saying her father needed a doctor.

There had been other instances that he wondered now if they were Callings. Times when he just knew what was wrong with a patient before he knew all the symptoms. Knew more than he should have about how to treat illnesses while he was in medical school. More than he should have, not having studied that particular aspect yet.

Vernon wondered if he should keep track of the feelings that could be Callings. That might help him recognize them when they came. It might help him avert some sort of trouble or more easily remedy what had occurred, like finding his father after the tornado.

He rolled onto his side. At least nothing terrible had happened to Lillian when they fell into the lake. Sure she had some stings that hurt and would itch for several days, but now she was home safe and sound in her apartment.

He had a bigger decision to think about. With her parents coming home, he needed to decide if he was going to ask Mr. Miller if he could court his daughter.

~~~~~

Lillian breathed a sigh of relief when the two male customers left the shop. They'd come in shortly after Will left to go home for lunch. He did so several times a week, bringing Pearl back with him for the afternoon. Lillian was always delighted to see her new sister-in-law. They'd chat, Pearl would help with customers, and crochet while Will worked on watches, other repairs and the commission for the rich businessman's wife's birthday. Lillian kept the books for the shop and had a small desk where the ledgers were kept.

The men had inquired about several pieces of jewelry. They looked at every locket in the display case. They were polite, but something set Lillian on edge. She wasn't fond of men coming in while Will was gone. Maybe she'd suggest they close the shop for lunch hour.

Lillian had watched the men carefully as they looked at each locket. It seemed as if they were inspecting the shop as well as the piece one or the other was holding. When they said they'd think about which one to purchase and come back later, she'd agreed that was a good idea since they were so unsure.

When they closed the door as they left, Lillian locked it and placed the sign indicating the shop would open again in a half an hour. She needed the time to settle her nerves.

~~~~~

Lillian watched Pearl and Will as the family waited for the train to arrive. She could tell they both were nervous. She wished they'd written telling their parents about the marriage. That could blow up in their faces like a dynamite explosion. Neither parent was going to be happy about the situation. She knew Pearl had no clue about the shop. Will should have told her about that too. No matter now. Will was in big trouble and she just wanted to not be anywhere around when the explosion occurred.

The train pulled to a stop with noise and steam. Lillian saw her parents stepping onto the platform and followed the grandchildren as they ran to greet them. It wasn't long after hugs and kisses before one of the older ones spilled the beans.

"Uncle Will got married to Aunt Pearl while you were gone. We got to go to the wedding. It was fun."

Matthew and Luella straightened and stared straight at Will and Pearl. Uh oh. They weren't happy. Lillian didn't blame them, but she wanted to defuse the situation and she wanted to hug her parents. They'd been gone two months and Lillian had missed them terribly. Mary had tried to fill the gap but she wasn't Mother.

Lillian moved forward and was enveloped in loving arms. "I missed you both so much. I'm so glad you are home. You'll have to tell me everything." She looked up at her father. "Did you bring me a present?"

That brought a laugh from both of her parents. It was the same question she'd always asked the times her father went on business trips. "Yes, squirt, I did. Or should I say your mother did. We brought presents for everyone."

Lillian stepped aside so Mary and Josey could welcome the couple home. She watched as Matthew and Luella greeted Will and Pearl. The stilted congratulations they offered weren't very genuine. When Will and Matthew went to gather the luggage with Clyde and Fred, Lillian rushed to Pearl's side.

"Mother, you won't believe how beautiful the wedding gown Pearl has made is. I'm sure she'll be getting many more commissions once it's seen at the Clary wedding."

"I'm sure it is lovely. You have a real talent for making lace, Pearl. I look forward to seeing it." Her mother's tone wasn't welcoming to her new daughter-in-law.

They saw the rest of the family head off in their new motorcars, taking their parents home. Tonight, they'd all have supper at Mary and Clyde's and Will and Pearl would have to face the disapproval of the elder Millers.

CHAPTER EIGHT

"Please Vernon, please. Just a little lesson. Just enough so I can say I've driven a car." Lillian stood beside him on the sidewalk. She was begging with her hands clasped together, big puppy dog eyes. Her pouty lips made him want to kiss them. She'd been begging ever since he'd gotten the car. It was cute but getting a little tiresome. Maybe if he let her drive once, way out in the country where she couldn't run into anything, she would be satisfied and quit with the begging.

Vernon tapped her on the nose. "Since we are going out in the country, I'll show you how. But you have to listen to what I tell you and do just as I say."

Because of a rare day off, they were having an opportunity to spend some time together in the middle of the week. Will had given

Lillian the time off, though how he could have kept her from going, he didn't know. The trees were starting to turn colors so they were going to look at their beauty. A picnic basket was in the backseat along with a blanket for them to sit on.

Lillian clapped her hands and flung her arms around him, jumping in her excitement. "Let's go. You can tell me all about how on the way." She wrenched the door open and climbed in without his assistance. At least she was still on the passenger side.

When he got behind the wheel, she had scooted closer, which suited him just fine. "I'm not sure if you could start the engine. It takes some strength. You see, I leave it on when I'm going to only be away a short time. Once we have you driving, I may have you try to start it, but let's concentrate on the driving right now."

As they drove through the city, Vernon explained how to shift into and change gears. He hoped she was able to do so smoothly, since he didn't want the gears to grind.

"Oh, my, it's much more complicated than I thought. Two levers and three pedals. It's going to take me some time to figure out which does what." Lillian was leaning down, studying his feet. "I thought all you had to do was make it go and turn the steering wheel.

"We'll go over it again when you are sitting here." Vernon hoped she was a quick study. He didn't want to spend all day showing her how to drive. He was sure it was going to wreck his nerves.

They left town and headed into the countryside. The fall day was warm with not a cloud in the sky. Vernon had the top folded down. Trees lined the road and bracketed the fields being harvested. Reds, yellows, oranges, and browns dotted the green of the trees. Monarch butterflies, white and yellow swallowtail butterflies, and even a few blue morpho butterflies flitted around and in front of the motorcar. Bluebirds, red winged blackbirds, meadowlarks, goldfinches added their songs to the rustle of leaves.

"Doesn't that hay smell wonderful?" Lillian took a deep breath. "So fresh and clean."

Vernon took glimpses of her face as they drove along. She'd tipped her face to the sun and closed her eyes. She was so lovely. So sweet. So full of life. He decided then and there that he would meet with Mr. Miller and ask permission to court Lillian. Not that he hadn't been, but he hadn't truly made up his mind that Lillian was who he wanted to spend his life with.

Marriage was a covenant between a man, woman, and God. It was for a lifetime. He'd courted a few ladies in the past who he knew very quickly he'd not want to live with one day, let alone an entire lifetime. Lillian brought excitement into his life. Sometimes a little too much enthusiasm, but that was okay. He loved the joy she had for life. Yes, she was the woman he wanted by his side.

She was the woman he'd fallen in love with. When it happened, he didn't know. The first time he saw her, Vernon had known she would be part of his life. He just hadn't realized how large a part she would play.

Now, he needed to convince her father he was worthy of his youngest child.

~~~~~

"Are you ready for me to drive?" Lillian looked up at Vernon. There was a light in his eyes that made her want to be kissed. He normally gave her a sweet, short kiss when he took her home. She wanted more, but knew he was being a gentleman just as she'd want a beau to be.

She desperately wanted to move on with her life. As much as she enjoyed working at the shop, she wanted a husband and family. Most of her school friends were married and beginning families. She felt like she was being left behind.

Was Vernon interested in making a life with her? Did he have more than friendly affection for her? Did he feel for her what she felt for him? Lillian didn't want to put a name to her feelings. She was afraid that if she did, and he didn't, her heart would break.

Vernon laughed at her question. "Sweetheart, I'll never be ready for you to drive." Belying his words, Vernon pulled to the side of the road. "You slide over here and I'll go around and sit next to you."

Lillian scooted and grabbed the steering wheel. A wide smile broke out on her face. She turned the wheel a bit. "Oh, the steering is harder than I thought it would be."

"I have a feeling, everything is going to be harder than you think." He sat close to her, just as she had. "This lever on the right is the throttle. When you want to go, you pull it back. No, not yet!!!" He placed his hand over hers. "Let me go over what everything does first then we'll take it step by step."

"Okay. This is the throttle." She tapped the lever.

"This lever is the handbrake." Vernon pointed to the lever sticking up out of the floor to the left of the steering wheel. "It's what puts the car in gear. Low speed is in the middle. High speed is at the top."

"Handbrake. Got it."

"This pedal," he pointed to the right most of the three on the floor, "is the brake. When you want to stop, you press it down."

"I thought the handbrake would stop the car. Isn't that what a brake does on a carriage? You pull the brake, and it makes the wheels stop turning."

"Well, yes, but here you push the pedal. When you stop you pull the handbrake back and it locks the wheels. When you push it forward, it allows the gears to engage and make the motor run so you can move."

"Isn't the motor running now? I can hear it, and the car is vibrating."

"Yes, it is running in idle. The gears that make the tires turn aren't engaged so it won't move. The handbrake releases the tires so they can turn and engages the gears."

"Okay, what's the middle pedal for? It's higher than the other ones." Lillian tapped it with her toe.

"You press it when you want to go in reverse."

"Oh, do you use it very often?"

"Only when I have to back the car up. Just like with horses, sometimes you need to back up so you can get to where you can move forward."

"Will I have to back up?" Lillian wasn't sure she would be able to without hitting something.

"No, you'll just go forward or stop. If we have to go backwards, I'll do it."

"Good." Lillian let out a relieved breath."

"That pedal on the left, it's the clutch. You push it when you want to make the car move and when you want the motor to run at a different speed."

"Huh? I thought the throttle controlled the speed." Lillian was confused.

"It does, but when you want to go at a higher speed, you need to change the gears to a different set. You do that when the motorcar is going faster. It makes the motor run better. I'm not sure of the technical explanation. Just know that when you get going, you need to press the clutch and shift the handbrake all the way forward."

"I thought I did that when I wanted to move."

"Yes, but you only move it half way forward. That's for idling and low gear. When you want to be in high gear, it has to be all the way up."

"This is complicated."

"Well, it does take some getting used to. It took me a while to get on to everything."

"Can I try now?" Lillian gave a little bounce. Even though she wasn't sure about what everything did, she was ready to drive.

"I think that covers everything. Oh, when you want to move the handbrake, you need to squeeze the release and push it half way forward. Put your right foot on the brake pedal."

Lillian found that her palms were sweaty. Luckily her gloves absorbed the dampness. She pressed the pedal and grabbed the lever, squeezed and pushed. It moved, and she stopped pushing where Vernon had told her.

"Now, press the far left pedal, the clutch, with your left foot. At the same time lift your right foot slowly to release the brake."

Lillian tried to do as he said. The car lurched forward and she pushed the brake down again. She lifted her right foot and the car lurched again. "My, this is much more difficult than I thought."

~~~~~

Vernon ran a hand around the back of his neck. He wondered if all the jerking was going to damage both his and Lillian's. The first five minutes she'd been driving, or more correctly trying to drive, had been nothing but jerking and lurching forward a few feet until she became comfortable with releasing the brake pedal. They'd gone about twenty feet along the straight road.

She'd killed the motor four times, so he'd had to crank it again to start it. Lillian did learn how to start the engine and even cranked it once. She decided she'd rather drive than start the car.

She let the clutch go and the car slowed to a stop. "Why did it stop?"

"You let off the clutch. When you are in low gear you have to keep the clutch pedal depressed." Vernon licked his lips. They'd become dry. His mouth was too. Lillian had told him they had a jar of lemonade in the picnic basket. He was hoping she would tire of trying to drive soon so they could have their lunch.

She pressed the clutch again and the car lurched forward. "I think I have it now. Can I go faster?"

Not what Vernon wanted to do, but if she was going to learn, he had to let her increase the speed.

"We'll go a little faster. You pull the throttle back…"

Lillian grabbed the handle and yanked it down. The motor roared and lurched ahead. She pulled her foot off the clutch and they slowed.

Vernon pushed it back up part way, slowing the engine. "Slowly, you don't want to kill the engine." He didn't tell her that he didn't want her to go very much faster. "Just a few notches at a time." He pointed to the narrow notches on the throttle plate. "Each one increases or decreases the speed of the engine. You want to only move it one or two at a time, especially when you are learning.

Lillian took a deep breath and let it out. "I'm ready." She pushed the clutch and the car began to move. Letting go of the wheel with her right hand she eased the throttle lever down two notches. The speed of the car increased a little. "That's better."

They bounced along the bumpy road. Vernon looked at Lillian. She was smiling. Her eyes sparkled. He could almost guess her thoughts. She was getting over her nervousness and enjoying herself.

A tire hit a rut and the steering wheel jerked right. Vernon grabbed and steadied it while Lillian pulled her foot off the clutch.

"Oh, my. That wasn't very fun."

Vernon laughed. "No, that's another thing you need to learn, how to steer around holes and ruts and bumps. This road is actually very good. The ruts aren't very deep. Some of the roads I've been on are terrible. They are dirt so when it rains, they become mud. Not only does it get all over the car, but it's very easy to get stuck in the mud. I usually take my horse or horse and buggy if it's rained. Much easier not to get stuck. It's hard to unstick a motorcar."

"I need to back the throttle off to start going again, don't I?" Lillian asked.

"Yes, unless you want to crank again." Vernon grinned at her.

"No, thank you." Primly she adjusted the throttle and a little more smoothly, set the car in motion.

There was a curve in the road and Lillian tried to turn the wheel to go around it. First, she tried to turn too soon and had to pull the wheel the other way. That resulted in over steering and she had to turn the wheel back. They zigzagged around the curve, releasing a nervous breath when she was straight on the road again.

"Well, that was interesting. You never said a thing to help me."

Vernon swallowed. "You were doing fine, or at least okay. My giving instructions while you were trying to steer would have made you more nervous. You got us around the curve without taking us into a ditch. I would have helped steer if we were in danger of leaving the road."

Lillian released the clutch and allowed the vehicle to glide to a stop. She turned to him. Her eyes were bright. "Thank you, Vernon. I appreciate you teaching me to drive. I do believe I'm done for today. You may change places with me." She laid a hand on his arm. "I don't think any other person would trust me enough to teach me to drive their automobile. You haven't a clue as to how much this means to me."

Vernon saw that her eyes were full. He wondered at her words, that no one would trust her to learn to drive. Or to teach her. He leaned forward and kissed her. "It was my pleasure. Well, at least most of the time. I'm not sure my neck will ever be the same though."

"Oh, you," Lillian laughed and swatted at him as he quickly exited the passenger side to walk around, replacing her behind the wheel.

CHAPTER NINE

Lillian shook her head. She couldn't believe her mother had acted like that toward Pearl and didn't understand why Will was angry at her. Hopefully, what Lillian had said, and Luella realized, would help them reconcile.

At least Lillian knew why Pearl was so quiet if Luella was at the shop. It seemed that Pearl would sort of fade into the background and silently crochet. She wouldn't come out of her shell until Luella left.

Lillian had invited her mother to stay for lunch after they'd discussed Will's objection to how she was treating his wife. It had been a rather quiet lunch. Once the dishes were done, her mother left. Now, Lillian could do the shopping she wanted to do.

Putting on her coat and pinning a hat on her head, Lillian left the shop and hurried over to Townsend and Wyatt Dry Goods store. They'd just begun carrying clothing suitable for driving or riding in an automobile. She was tired of getting dust on her clothing, in her hair and eyes.

She went straight to the department where they were sold and looked over the styles. Lillian wanted one that could be worn during inclement weather. Winter was coming and she didn't want to miss going with Vernon or the chance to practice her driving. She chose a loose, long, tan coat with waterproof rubber coating.

The hat was wide with a flat crown and brim. Under the brim was cloth that gathered around the hair to keep the dust away. A scarf tied under the chin held the hat on and could also be used to shield the face. Not wanting to cover her face if she drove, Lillian bought driving goggles, laughing at how she looked when she saw herself in the mirror.

The items were expensive since driving was still more of a luxury than common. She didn't drop her package as she passed Mr. Dimmick, manager of the department, as she had done when Pearl worked at the store. He grinned at her and gave her a little salute as she left.

As she walked back to the shop, a man was leaning against the building across the street. When she neared his line of sight, he straightened and tipped his hat.

Lillian thought he might be one of the two men who had made her so uneasy when they came into the shop after Will had left for lunch. Then again, she couldn't really see his face since it was in the shadow of a wide brimmed hat. His clothing was different also, but that wasn't unusual. Not acknowledging his action, she picked up her pace and got her key out of her pocket before she got to the shop door.

When Lillian was back in her apartment, she tried the entire ensemble on and studied herself in the mirror. Pleased with the effect, Lillian felt she was readier than ever to drive Vernon's motorcar. Hopefully, the weather would allow her to do so often before the roads turned to mud with the winter weather coming.

~~~~~

Vernon wiped his hands on his pants to get the sweat off. His hands were clammy. He was sitting in Mr. Miller's den at his home. Vernon had arranged to meet with Lillian's father at his last office appointment. At that time, Mr. Miller looked Vernon up and down, nodded, and set the time and date.

"Mrs. Miller will be in with coffee and pumpkin pie shortly. Let's wait until we are private again before we discuss what it is that has brought you here." Matthew folded his hands on the blotter covering most of the large oak desk.

Vernon swallowed and nodded. He looked around the room. It was comfortable, masculine, bookcases lined one wall. The desk was set in front of large windows facing the side yard. Two upholstered chairs were arranged around a small table off to the side. Vernon wished they were sitting in those rather than across the desk from each other. They would be on more of an even footing for what he wanted to ask. But, he supposed Mr. Miller wanted to be sure Vernon understood his position as Lillian's father and protector. He did have all the power here. If the man didn't want Vernon courting his daughter, that would put paid to what Vernon wanted.

Mrs. Miller came in, carrying a silver tray with a coffee service and two pieces of pie. "Here you go. I'll pour, then leave you gentlemen to your discussion." She served, then smiled at him as she left, closing the door behind her.

Matthew cleared his throat. "I don't suppose you are here to talk about my health."

"No, sir." Vernon took a sip of coffee to wet his suddenly dry throat. "I'm sure Lil… Miss Miller wrote to you about she and I spending time together while you were in Arkansas."

Matthew's lips twitched, indicating he was aware of Vernon starting to use Lillian's first name. "Yes, she wrote of you rather often."

"Um, as you know, my profession will enable me to make quite a good living."

"Yes, I've received bills for your services."

A lump formed in Vernon's throat. Maybe it wasn't a good idea to remind him of that. "Ah, yes, um, Lil… Miss Miller is a lovely young lady."

"She is lovely. She takes after her mother."

"I've gotten to know her well over the past few months. She, Will, and Pearl, er, Mrs. Will Miller and I have spent several days and evenings together allowing us to become better acquainted."

"So she indicated in her letters."

Vernon rubbed his palms along his pant legs again. This was much harder than he'd thought it would be. Mr. Miller wasn't making it any easier with his short statements with no follow-up. He took a deep breath. "Not only is she lovely to look at, but she is beautiful in spirit too."

Matthew chuckled. "Very nicely put. She has a spark within her, that's for sure. Always has had."

The laughter eased Vernon's nervousness. Surely, if Mr. Miller wasn't going to approve of his suit, the man wouldn't be laughing.

"Sir, I've come to care a great deal for your daughter." Vernon plunged on before his nervousness returned. "I'd like your permission to formally court Miss Miller." There, he'd said it.

Matthew sat silent, staring at Vernon for a long moment, making him squirm in his chair. "Seems to me that you've been doing a fair amount of courting already."

"Um, I suppose you could say that. To be totally truthful, I have been attracted to her since we met. Will and I struck up a friendship, allowing me to be around Miss Miller. We've gone on some outings, both with Will and his wife, before they were married, and since. We've also been together without anyone along. I've been very careful not to compromise her reputation. I will continue to do so."

"I appreciate that. It's a bit awkward with her living by herself above the shop." Matthew poured more coffee into his cup and lifted it to offer to refill Vernon's, which he did at his nod.

Somewhat unsure, Vernon cleared his throat. "Are you approving my request, sir?"

Matthew waved his hand as he took a drink. "Yes, I do suppose I didn't really make that clear. I knew what you wanted when you asked for this meeting at my last appointment. I told Luella about it, and we both agree you'll be a good husband to her. She needs someone who can corral her when she goes off over excited about things. I believe you can do that. Will let me know of your interaction with her. That you can tell her 'no' and stick to your guns. Not all men could do that."

All the tension left Vernon and he couldn't suppress the smile that broke across his face. "Thank you, sir, thank you. You can't know how happy that makes me."

"Vernon, I've been through this with two other daughters. You've handled it better than either Clyde or Fred. Poor Fred, he stumbled and stammered through the whole thing."

They both laughed, then Vernon began to bring up something that had been mentioned earlier. "Mr. Miller..."

"Call me Matthew," he interrupted. "You can call Lillian by her name. I know you have for a long time. She wrote about you four using your first names. Now, there's no reason to stand on ceremony. You can even call Luella by her name, though I suggest you ask her first. She'll approve of you even more if you do."

"Thank you, Matthew. As you mentioned before, Lillian living alone and us courting could create issues with her reputation. Do you think she would be willing to move back here until we settle the matter between us? I'm not prepared to make a declaration to her more than I want to court her. I live in a very small apartment. It's not even as big as the one above the shop. I'd like to have the time to find a house. I'd also like to have her input once we get to that point."

Matthew rubbed his chin. "How long do you plan on courting her before you declare yourself?"

"I'm thinking possibly Christmas. I have some prospects of joining several other doctors in a partnership. We are working out the details. If it comes together, the area and value of the home I could purchase for Lillian would be better. That's why I'd like to wait a while before proposing. I don't want to look for a house that might be beyond my capacity to afford. By December, it should all be settled."

"Good thinking," Matthew said. "The difficulty is that Lillian and her mother were fighting like cats and dogs before Lillian up and moved in with Will. She didn't even ask him. I don't want to live in that sort of stress again. I'm sure it wouldn't be advantageous to my health."

"No, it wouldn't. What do you suggest?"

"I'd say you, Lillian, Luella, and I go out to dinner to honor your commitment to court. I can suggest she move home for propriety's sake. You can warn both ladies that the stress of arguing will be harmful to my health. That it might bring on another episode that could be more serious than my other one."

Vernon smiled. "A very good idea, sir. Very good indeed."

CHAPTER TEN

Lillian didn't think a day could get drearier. It was cold, windy, and rain was beating on the windows. Will had left the shop early since not a single person had come in all day. Lillian didn't blame them. She wouldn't want to be out on a day like today either. To top that off, Vernon hadn't called or come by in two days.

She knew he was busy. He was a doctor after all. Several people she knew were going to him and had told her how good he was. He seemed to be able to diagnose more quickly than some of the other doctors. He was getting a reputation for being gentle, kind, and respectful. Some physicians were none of those things. Vernon was.

Deciding to just close the shop, Lillian began moving the jewelry to the safe. It wouldn't take her long, she'd done this job every day since she'd started working.

Tonight was going to be a long one. Without Will or Pearl living with her, the evenings seemed to stretch. She was only cooking for herself now. Several times a week Will went home to have lunch with Pearl, so she didn't even have to fix him lunch.

Lillian locked the safe and trudged up the stairs to her empty apartment. She was lonely. There was no way she'd tell anyone that. First, she didn't want pity. Didn't want anyone to know that she felt left behind and left out of moving forward in life. Second, she didn't want anyone to know she sort of, maybe more than a little, wanted to move home. Being alone every evening made even bickering with her mother appealing.

Filling the tea kettle, she set it on the stove to heat. There were leftovers she'd reheat for her supper. There always seemed to be leftovers now.

Lillian went into her bedroom and looked around. She twisted her lips to the side. The room was a mess. She hadn't made her bed. Her towel was askew on the rod on the wall.

Several pairs of shoes were scattered around on the floor, some partially hidden by a petticoat. More petticoats, a chemise, and stockings littered the floor and a chair. The middle drawer of her dresser was open with something hanging over the edge. Since Pearl had moved out, Lillian's housekeeping had definitely disintegrated.

Lillian sighed and began removing her clothes. She was going to get into her nightgown. Why stay dressed when she was all alone? She'd get comfortable. No corset. No garters holding up her stockings.

Once she'd changed, she began picking up. The kettle began to whistle. She'd have a cup of tea, then come back to work on the disaster of her room.

Lillian picked up the kettle and turned to get a tea cup. The leg of the chair she hadn't pushed back under the table caught her foot and the knob on the back, the wide sleeve of her nightgown. She tripped, the boiling water pouring from the spout spilled down the arm she reached out to stop her fall with, and on her leg as she stumbled.

She hit the floor, the kettle escaping from her hand and spilling the hot liquid. Lillian cried out in pain. All she wanted to do was curl up in a ball to protect her burned skin, but knew she had to get away from the steaming water lest she be burned worse.

Stumbling to the bathroom, she plugged the bathtub and began running the cold water. The nightgown landed in a wet heap on the floor as she flung it off and crawled into the cold water.

Lillian hissed in a breath through her teeth as the water hit the burns. Tears were blinding her as they filled her eyes and flowed down her cheeks. Her arm was red and blisters were forming. Her leg didn't look much better.

As the water rose, its coolness eased some of the agony. She was shivering but didn't get out until the pain of her left arm and leg was tolerable. She had to get out, dress in something, and get help. That meant going down the stairs to the telephone.

Lillian pulled the plug and sat in the tub until the water drained away. It was going to hurt to climb out. She'd have to use her burned arm and leg.

"Okay, let's do this." Lillian grabbed the side of the tub with her unburned right hand

and turned over, pulling her right knee up so she was kneeling on it. Her burned left leg bumped on the side of the tub, making her cry out.

By the time she struggled out, Lillian was sobbing in pain. She toweled dry as well as she could and limped to her bedroom. A weak laugh came out as she saw her dressing gown hanging on the tall bedpost. At least she didn't have to go clear to the wardrobe to fetch it. Her slippers were on the floor nearby.

More pain shot through her arm as she put it through the sleeve of the gown. At least she was able to button it up with only one hand. Now, all she had to do was go all the way down the stairs to the telephone. She planned to call Will. She wanted her mother, but didn't want to scare them. Didn't want her father to have another spell.

As she reached the bottom step, the telephone rang. Lillian lifted a prayer of thanks. At least she wouldn't have to pretend nothing was wrong when she spoke with the operator to connect the call.

"Hello?" she croaked out as she put the receiver to her ear.

"Lillian, are you okay?" It was Vernon.

"No, burned. Please come help me."

"I'm on my way. Just stay there."

Lillian heard the click as he hung up. She slid down the wall, letting the receiver hang on the end of its cable. Tears coursed down her cheeks. She'd wait until he banged on the door before she got up to answer it.

~~~~~

Something was wrong. Vernon was having a Calling, but it wasn't clear enough to identify. He just knew that someone who was dear to him was in trouble and needing him. Who was it? He prayed for God to let him know who. He paced his apartment and looked out the window. Rain continued to hit the window though he couldn't see because night had fallen. He wasn't going to wait. He was going to start calling his family and friends.

He lifted the earpiece and clicked for an operator. "Plaza 8585, please." He'd check on Lillian first. Then he'd call Will. He hoped it wasn't either of them, but especially Pearl. It was far too early for her to give birth.

"Hello?"

Vernon could hardly recognize Lillian's voice. His heart tightened in his chest. It was her. She was who his Calling had been for.

"Lillian, are you okay?"

"No, burned. Please come help me."

"I'm on my way. Just stay there." He hung up the receiver and clicked for the operator again. He called Will and told him about his call to Lillian. Vernon hung up, grabbed his coat, hat, and medical bag, and flew out of his apartment and down the stairs.

"Please, Lord, make the motorcar start. Keep her safe until I can get there. Help me do what's best while I treat her."

Vernon threw his bag onto the seat, set the timing and pulled out the choke. Grabbing the handle, he cranked. The engine started on the first turn. "Thank you, Lord." He drove a little too fast for the wet streets, and was glad there weren't others out on such a rainy night.

When he parked by the shop, the lights were off, the place dark. Lillian had been downstairs when he'd called. Surely, she still was. He'd told her to stay there.

The blind had been pulled down on the door so he couldn't see in. Vernon pounded on the door. Will shouldn't be very much behind him as he'd purchased a motorcar not long ago.

"Coming." Lillian's voice told of her pain.

A light came on, the lock turned, and she pulled the door open. Vernon didn't wait. "Step back." He pushed the door wider so he could enter.

Lillian stood, bent over, her hair wet and dangling around her face.

"What happened? Where are you hurt?" Vernon didn't touch her as he didn't want to chance touching the burn.

"Left arm and leg. Tripped with the tea kettle."

Now that he knew where she was injured, he picked her up carefully with her right side against his chest. He carried her to the stairs. "Will is coming. I called him. Let's get you upstairs where I can examine and treat your burns."

Lillian laid her head on his shoulder and released a deep sigh. "I'm so glad you're here. I was going to call for help when you called."

The shop door opened with a bang. "Lillian, Vernon," Will shouted.

"Just going upstairs," Vernon answered. By the time he reached the top, both Will and Pearl were right behind him.

Pearl scooted around them and entered Lillian's bedroom. She pulled the covers to the end of the bed. Vernon laid her gently on the mattress.

"What happened?" Pearl asked.

"I tripped with a boiling kettle. Spilled on my arm and leg." Lillian said softly.

Vernon lifted the side of her dressing gown away from her leg. Pearl tucked the other side under her right leg, making sure it was covered.

The leg was red with some blistering from above the knee nearly to her ankle. Some of the blisters were open and damp, probably from rubbing against the fabric of her robe.

"I'm going to have to cut the sleeve to see the arm, Lillian." Vernon opened his bag and took out his scissors. She'd closed her eyes, so she just nodded.

When the arm was exposed, he saw the burns ran from just below her elbow to the back of her hand. They were similar to the ones on her leg. Open and oozing.

They appeared to be severe first degree burns since the blisters were small. That meant less chance of scarring so long as infection didn't set in. He cleaned and dressed the wounds with Pearl's help. Will had gone to get her parents. Vernon knew she wanted her mother. Lillian had said so several times.

To help her sleep and reduce her pain, Vernon gave her laudanum. When she was peaceful, he went into the kitchen where Pearl was.

"There was water all over the floor and the kettle over there." She pointed. "I've mopped up the water. How badly is she going to scar?" Pearl's eyes were bright with tears.

"If we can keep them from getting infected, it should be minimal. The burns weren't deep. She must have been able to cool them off quickly." Vernon sat down in one of the chairs around the table.

"I found a couple of towels on the floor in the bathroom. Maybe she was able to cool them in the bath." Pearl sat down across from him.

They heard the shop door open and fast moving steps came up the stairs. Luella entered the apartment just as Vernon and Pearl entered the parlor.

"Where's Lillian? Where's my baby?" That she'd been crying was evident on her face. "How badly burned is she?"

Matthew entered behind her along with Will.

"She has severe first degree burns on her left arm and leg. I've bandaged them with butter in the cloths. If I had some lime water and oil, I'd apply that, but I won't be able to get it until tomorrow. They'll need to be treated often to keep infection out and lessen any scarring." He went on explaining how they should be tended. "She's sleeping. I gave her some laudanum. She shouldn't be left alone tonight."

"Oh, we'll stay, Vernon. No doubt about that." Matthew's use of his given name had both Will and Pearl looking at him.

"I also think she shouldn't stay here by herself. She's going to be in a lot of pain and the burns will need to be treated several times a day. Do you think Lillian would be willing to move to your home?" Vernon asked.

"We'll see that she does," Luella said. "Do you know what happened? How this occurred?"

"She said she was carrying a hot tea kettle and tripped." Vernon glanced toward the bedroom. He wanted to go sit beside her in case she woke up. It was silly. He knew she would sleep for several hours.

They sat in the parlor for a while. Will and Pearl decided to go home. There was nothing they could do. Pearl would help tend Lillian whenever Luella and Matthew wanted.

Vernon didn't want to leave, though he knew Lillian was in no danger and in good hands with her parents staying.

Matthew cleared his throat. "You haven't asked Lillian if you can court her yet, have you?" The tone was neutral, not critical or humorous.

"No, sir. I haven't had the chance. I was on call and there were several emergencies I was asked to help with. I haven't had the time to come or even to telephone her for several days. I was planning to on our outing on Saturday evening. I guess that won't happen."

The thought made his stomach ache. He wanted to let Lillian know he was serious about her. He wanted to share the opportunity for the partnership with her. Let her know his intent. That would be delayed at least for a few days.

"Well, I suppose the only positive aspect of this is that she'll move home without much fuss," Luella said. "That will make your courting of her much easier and more proper." She smiled at him. "Not the way I wanted to encourage her to return home, but at least she'll come home without argument."

~~~~~

"Oooh," Lillian moaned. She hurt. Her arm and leg felt as if they were on fire. She shifted her right leg, trying to get comfortable.

"Lillian, how can I help?" The voice was her mother's.

Lillian opened her eyes. The room was dimly lit by an oil lamp with the wick set low. "Mama." It would be okay. Her mother would take care of her. She closed her eyes.

"You haven't called me that since you were little." Lillian could hear the smile in her mother's voice.

"I hurt. The burns."

"I know, sweetheart. Vernon is fixing a few drops of laudanum for you."

"He called, Mama. Just before I was going to call someone for help. He called and then he came. Will and Pearl too."

"Yes, Will came and got your father and me."

She nodded. A shadow fell over her. Lillian opened her eyes again and saw her father. She tried to give him a grin but failed when a stab of pain flared.

"You're going to be fine, Vernon says." Her father leaned down and brushed his hand over her hair. "It will take a while, but you'll recover completely."

"Just like you. Can I take trip to Arkansas to recuperate?" Lillian was able to give a half grin at her teasing.

"That's my girl." Vernon stepped into the bedroom. "Always looking to make an adventure out of everything. No, you can't take a trip. At least not for a while. I have to be around to change your dressings. I'm going to do that now. Then you are going to have some of the lovely soup your mother made. After that, some laudanum to help you sleep."

Lillian turned her lip up in a snarl. "Yuck. That stuff tastes terrible."

"It's medicine. It's supposed to." Matthew said. "Come, Luella, let's get the soup ready while Vernon changes her dressings."

When they'd left the room, Lillian looked at Vernon as he began cutting the bandages off. She wanted to ask if she truly was his girl, but didn't want him to say she wasn't.

She looked at the wound when he lifted off the wrappings. "Ooh, no wonder I hurt so much. That looks terrible."

"It does, but they aren't deep. You must have cooled them off quickly."

"I wanted to curl up on the floor but there was hot water everywhere. I got into the bathtub with cold water. I sat in there until I was so cold I was trembling. Then I got out, dried off a little, and got into my dressing gown. I was just coming downstairs when you called." She hissed in a breath when he began applying an ointment making her burn sting.

"Do you know about what time you injured yourself?" Vernon looked up from concentrating on his treatment.

She thought about it. "Maybe about quarter to six. Somewhere around there."

"I called about six-thirty. You must have stayed in the bath a long time. It helped keep the burns from deepening. You did the right thing."

"I was shivering too hard, I could barely climb out. All I knew is that I needed to cool off the burns and that was the only way I could do both at the same time."

Vernon finished dressing her arm and was beginning to cut the bandage off her leg when Luella and Matthew returned. Her father was carrying a tray with a mug and plate of buttered bread.

Luella looked at Lillian's leg. "Oh, my poor baby." Tears were filling her eyes.

"It looks worse than it is, but hurts more than that," Vernon says.

They arranged pillows behind Lillian so she was sitting up. Vernon worked on her leg, while she sipped soup from the mug. Luella sat on the edge of the bed. Matthew brought the chair close and sat down. Lillian noticed that her room had been picked up and blushed, embarrassed that they'd seen the mess.

When he finished, Vernon stood at the end of the bed and held one of the posts. "You're going to need care over the next while. My suggestion is that you move home, at least until you don't need the burns dressed several times a day. You won't be able to do that by yourself. You also won't be able to tend to daily chores."

Lillian turned to her mother. "Is that okay with you, Mother?" This fit into what she was wanting anyway. This way she wouldn't have to beg to come home because she was lonely. As stupid as she felt for having burned herself so badly, she was able to keep a bit of her dignity by not having to request to move home.

"Of course, sweetheart. We'll love to have you with us for as long as you want. Isn't that right, Matthew?"

"Of course." Matthew's eyes twinkled, and it seemed to Lillian there was more than her needing care in their desire to have her living with them.

When Lillian was finished with her soup and bread, Vernon gave her the laudanum and her mother gave her a glass of juice to wash away the taste.

"I'll leave now and come back in the morning to change the dressings." Vernon gave her hand a slight squeeze.

"You sleep now," Luella kissed her cheek. "Your father and I will stay here with you. If you need anything just call."

After they rearranged her pillows so she was reclining, Lillian yawned. "Thank you for coming." She snuggled down, turned on her unburned side, and mumbled, "Love you all."

CHAPTER ELEVEN

Vernon was surprised to find both Luella and Matthew at the jewelry shop. It was late in the afternoon, and he was planning on going to treat Lillian's burns once he was done with what he wanted to do here. Maybe he should wait until another day. He was a bit embarrassed to ask for help to purchase their daughter a birthday gift. It was awkward to let them know the price of his gift. He would be much more relaxed if it was only Will or Pearl waiting on him.

"Hello, Vernon. You haven't gone to treat Lillian yet, have you?" Luella asked, coming around the counter.

"No, ma'am. I'm planning on doing so once my business is done here." Vernon looked at Will, silently pleading with him to take over for his mother. Matthew was sitting at the workbench and gave him a little wave.

"What can I help you with?" Luella asked, smiling at him.

Vernon glanced at Will again, who rose from his chair.

"Mother, you were going to pack some more of Lillian's things. You know what she will want better than Father or me. Why don't you go do that while I help Vernon? Maybe he'll give you a ride home in his motorcar. You could take an extra box or two."

Vernon jumped on the idea. "Yes, I'd be glad to take you and Matthew home. Pack as many boxes as you want. We'll fit whatever you want in."

"Oh, thank you. I'll just go do that." Luella turned toward the stairs. "Come, Matthew, please help me with the packing. Once we're done, Will and Vernon can carry them down."

When they were alone, Will looked at Vernon with a smirk and raised eyebrow. "What can I help you with that you don't want my parents knowing about?"

Maybe Will wouldn't be much better if he was going to tease him. Vernon cleared his throat. "Lillian's birthday is coming up and I'd like to get her something. I was thinking of a locket."

Vernon could tell Will was surprised. "A birthday gift. Huh? Do my parents know about this?"

"About the birthday gift? No, but we've talked. I went to your father and asked to formally court Lillian."

"I was wondering when you were going to do so. Does Lillian know?" Will gave a small chuckle. "If she does, she's surely kept that secret better than she ever has before."

"I was going to ask her, but then she burned herself, so I've put it off. I will before her birthday. I want to be included in the family celebration. If I haven't made my intent known, there's no real reason for me to be."

Will nodded. Then he grinned wide. "Welcome to the family, brother. I couldn't have picked a better man for my sister than you. Let's take a look at the lockets I have." He took a black velvet lined tray from the display case. On it were lockets in yellow gold and white gold. Round, square, heart shaped, plain, engraved, and raised designs.

Vernon looked carefully at them, wondering how he was going to choose one. Then he saw it. A yellow gold locket with a raised stem of lilies. He picked it up and handed it to Will. "This one. A lily for my Lillian." He wanted to add the lily of his life, but kept the sentiment to himself. That was for him to share with Lillian.

"Very good choice. What chain do you want with it?" Will asked.

They decided on one and its length. Will tucked it into a box and wrapped it with white paper and tied a red ribbon around it. Vernon paid and hid the box in his pocket. He looked at the stairs, and, not hearing the Millers coming down, decided to address another matter with Will.

"I'd like for you to design a wedding ring set. Engagement and wedding ring for Lillian and a matching band for me."

"Aren't you getting the cart before the horse, here? You haven't even found out if she wants you to court her."

"I'm going to do that very soon. We can start on the design so that it's ready by the time I propose. I'm thinking of at Christmas time."

"We'll need to talk about what you want, before Lillian comes back to work." Will started to say something else but stopped as footsteps sounded on the stairs. "We'll get together, if not here, then you can come to supper some evening so Lillian or my parents won't get wind of it. My mother is nearly as bad as Lillian with keeping that kind of secret." He winked at Vernon.

Luella, followed by Matthew appeared at the bottom of the stairs. "So, did you conclude your business, Vernon?" Luella asked.

"Yes, I did. You cannot see it until Lillian does, but I'll tell you what it is. I bought a locket for her for her birthday. A small token of my affection for your daughter."

A smile and a pat on the shoulder preceded Luella's comment of, "You better ask her if she wants you to court her before then. You can't give it to her until you do. It wouldn't be proper."

"Yes, ma'am. You can be sure I will."

"You boys get those boxes brought down. I'm ready to go home and put my feet up,"

Matthew said, pointing to the stairs. "I'm still recovering, you know."

"Matthew, you've been using that excuse whenever you want your way. Please tell him he's healed so I can get him to do some things around the house," Luella teasingly whined.

"I'm not getting into that discussion." Vernon held up his hands in surrender. "I don't want to favor one future in-law over another."

While everyone laughed, he and Will headed up the stairs to get the boxes.

~~~~~

Lillian was bored. She wanted to get up and go downstairs to the parlor. At least she'd have a change of scenery. Today was the fourth day since she'd come home, and she hadn't left her room except to go to the bathroom. Vernon had been very strict in telling her to stay in bed until he told her she could leave it.

He'd been so sweet to her, other than his orders. Then he'd squinted his eyes at her and frowned. "There will be no more driving lessons for you if I find out you've not stayed right there." He'd pointed at her bed. Lillian had huffed at him, but stayed put.

Lillian leaned over and pulled the magazines she'd tossed across the covers to her. The pain from her burns had lessened over the days. Vernon came twice a day and changed the dressings. The lime-water and oil at least smelled good. It did tend to seep through the muslin wraps though.

Several times Vernon had called her his girl. She wondered if that meant more to her than he intended. He only called her that when her mother was around. His teasing about no more driving lessons if she left her bed. Did that mean he was planning to let her drive more? Or was he simply teasing her.

Before the accident, Vernon hadn't called or stopped by for several days. The absence made her question whether he wanted to continue seeing her in a serious sort of way. He hadn't, to her knowledge, spoken with her parents about any intentions that he might have. Nor had he hinted that he might.

Without looking at any of the magazines, she tossed them away again. Humph. Lillian started to cross her arms in frustration. The bandage on her left arm was wrapped from her bicep to her hand. It hampered bending her arm which was good since that would pull on her burn.

Bah! Lillian turned on her side, frustrated. She was so lonely, just lying here. Her parents had both gone to the shop after lunch. Maybe she'd try to take a nap, though all she'd done the last four days was rest and sleep.

A small brown bag landed in front of her, making her turn and look over her shoulder. Vernon stood in the doorway with a smile on his face. "I brought you a little something."

His smile and the gift brightened her day. Maybe only for a little while as he changed her dressings, but anything was better than lying here by herself. She pushed herself up against the headboard, her mother helping as she bustled into the room.

"Hello, my dear. Did you have a restful afternoon? Vernon came in to chat some with Will and brought us home in his motorcar. We were able to bring several more boxes of your things. I'll get them unpacked where you want them."

"Before we start on that, let me change the bandages," Vernon said. He placed his medical bag on the end of the bed and took out his scissors. Luella brought the tray holding the ointments and bandages kept in the room.

Lillian didn't like looking at the burns and hadn't watched for several days. When Vernon commented on how well they were healing, she studied them. The skin was still a bright pink but there were no blisters nor infection evident.

"They do look much better today. Do you think I can get out of this stupid bed? I'm so bored and tired of lying here," Lillian couldn't keep the petulance from her tone, earning her a sharp look from her mother.

"So, not even my gift, which you haven't even looked at, mind you, can raise your spirits?" Vernon gently washed the wounds, then smoothed ointment over them.

Lillian grabbed the small bag and opened it, one handed. "Oh, Vernon, how wonderful. Thank you so much. This definitely makes my day. Look, Mother." Lillian pulled a Tootsie Roll from the bag. "I haven't had these since the Fourth of July."

She took the end of the wrapping between her teeth and pulled on the other end. The paper untwisted revealing the chocolate nugget. Lillian took a bite and moaned in pleasure at the taste. "Want one?" she asked with her mouth full, as she held the bag up.

When Vernon was finished changing the dressings, he leaned down, pressing his fists onto the mattress. "If you promise to be a good girl and not do too much, I think you can begin normal activities. Not too much. Don't do anything that might damage the healing skin."

Lillian bounced and wrapped her arms around his neck. "I'll be good, I promise. Can I go down to supper tonight? I'm so sick of being in this bed."

Luella cleared her throat, making Lillian aware of her impropriety. Heat flushed her cheeks. She let Vernon go and settled herself back against the pillows.

"Yes, you can go down for supper. I'll go down and bring the boxes we brought up. Wait until the morning to unpack them."

"Yes, sir." Lillian saluted as he left the room. "Mother, help me decide what to wear."

"Let's pick something especially pretty. Your father invited Vernon to stay for supper."

Lillian threw the covers off and jumped out of bed. "I thought this day was simply awful. Now, it's just a wonderful day. Or at least late afternoon and evening."

CHAPTER TWELVE

Vernon held the chair for Lillian to be seated. They were at the Robidoux Hotel restaurant for supper, celebrating Lillian's release from staying at home. She was recovered enough to return to work at the shop.

He'd warned her to not tire herself. Half days for the next week, and if she became fatigued, she was to go upstairs and rest for a bit. Vernon didn't believe her promises to do so. He'd already warned Will and Pearl to make sure she complied.

Vernon leaned down as he pushed her chair in. "You look especially lovely tonight." The gown she wore was sapphire velvet with tan fur edging the yoke and collar. The velvet yoke was the color of the fur covered with sapphire Battenberg lace, which was echoed on the cuffs. The nipped in waist was also adorned with a belt matching the other trims. He knew he'd embarrassed her with his compliment when she dropped her head to arrange the napkin on her lap.

"Thank you," Lillian murmured.

The table they occupied was small. Vernon would be able to touch her face if he reached across. They were in a corner which gave them more privacy than more centrally located tables. The waiter came, took their orders, leaving them alone in the dimly lit corner.

Vernon seemed to be studying her, making Lillian nervous. He wouldn't bring her to such an expensive restaurant only to say he didn't want to see her anymore, would he? She played with her wine glass, twirling it by its stem, hoping Vernon wouldn't notice her anxiety.

"These plates are lovely, aren't they?" she asked making light conversation. "The red and gold pineapples and the Robidoux crest represent the hotel's reputation for hospitality."

Vernon only nodded. Lillian fell silent. Why was he staring at her so intently? Then, he straightened and leaned forward. He reached across the table and captured her fingers, stroking their backs with his thumb.

"Lillian, you have to know I'm attracted to you. I hope you reciprocate my feelings. I've spoken with your parents and gotten permission to inquire if you would be willing for me to formally court you. I'm doing so now. Will you allow me to?"

The earnestness in his face brought tears to Lillian's eyes. All she could do was nod. She'd been so afraid that he was just stringing her along. That her feelings for him were much stronger than his for her.

Lillian swallowed. "Yes, Vernon. I very willingly give my approval to your request." She stopped because a lump rose in her throat. When she was able to clear it, Lillian blinked away the tears and all her agitation evaporated. She grinned wickedly and leaned forward as she squeezed his hand. "Now you have to give me more driving lessons. It will prove your devotion to me."

A chuckle burst from Vernon. "We'll see. I may allow you to try again, but with winter coming, that may have to wait until spring. I haven't even driven in the snow or ice. I'm not trusting you with my motorcar in those conditions when I haven't mastered driving in them."

~~~~~

November blew in on a cold wind. The family celebrated Lillian's birthday on the Sunday before the actual day. They used their normal afternoon get together after church and held it at Matthew and Luella's house. Since the couple's return from Arkansas, they'd been rotating between Mary's, Josey's, and the home place for the gatherings. Will and Pearl were exempt since their house was too small to hold everyone, and with Pearl expecting, they didn't want to burden her with hosting.

Lillian was excited as it was also the first time Vernon would be attending. She'd telephoned her sisters about being formally courted and asked that they warn their husbands not to tease Vernon too badly. She didn't want him scared away from her crazy family.

Lillian and her mother had gone shopping and purchased a new gown for each of them. Neither woman was shy about having new clothes. Matthew simply smiled and paid the bills. He did wonder if Vernon knew what he was getting into with Lillian's penchants for 'needing' new garments. He did have to admit, both his ladies looked lovely as they entered the church. Vernon met them in the foyer, tucking Lillian's hand into the crook of his elbow.

Everyone was now assembling at the Miller house. Every family contributed to the meal. Lillian left Vernon to the tender mercies of the men, going to help in the kitchen. When the entire family was seated around the large dining table Matthew rose to stand at the head of the table.

"Since Lillian has never been able to keep anything to herself, I know you all have heard that she is being formally courted by Dr. Vernon Strasser. Her mother and I have confidence the relationship will grow and blossom. We welcome him to our table and fellowship.

"We are celebrating that today, as well as Lillian's birthday." He focused his loving gaze upon her. "My dear, you have grown into a charming, beautiful lady on both the outside as well as inside." His eyes took on a teasing twinkle. "You may thank your mother and me for all of that."

Everyone at the table laughed, even the children who didn't understand their Papa's speech. Lillian's cheeks turned a pretty pink. Vernon, holding her hand under the table, gave hers a squeeze.

Just as Matthew was going to continue speaking, a little voice from the children's end of the table called out, "Can we eat now?"

His speech cut short amidst laugher, Matthew said grace and began passing the large platter of pot roast.

After the meal everyone moved to the parlor to watch Lillian open her presents. The children grouped themselves in front of her so they wouldn't miss anything. They were excited about the presents and the birthday cake that would be served after the opening.

When Lillian opened the locket from Vernon, she touched it with her finger. "Lilies, my favorite. Help me put it on."

Vernon did and then looked into her eyes. Lillian's breath was taken away. He may not have said the words to her, but his love for her was written all over his face. She couldn't pull her gaze from his. The sounds of those in the room faded. Time seemed to still. Then, Mary's husband, Clyde broke the spell.

"Kiss her already."

Lillian's eyes went wide as Vernon did just that.

~~~~~

Lillian wasn't going to be at the shop in the afternoon, so Vernon leapt up the steps as soon as he finished seeing his last patient for the day. If the rings were going to be finished for Christmas, he and Will needed to complete the designs. It was only a few weeks until Thanksgiving. He knew it might take some time to get the correct gems.

Pearl was helping a customer, and waved him to come back behind the counter. She knew what he was there for. He'd gone to supper at Will and Pearl's house earlier in the week. They'd discussed Vernon's ideas and Will had made preliminary sketches. Today, he'd see the final drawings and decide on the size of the stones.

"Hi, Will. You can't believe how nervous I am about this. It's such a big decision. What if she doesn't like them?"

Will laughed. "I don't think you have anything to worry about on that score. They will be beautiful. She will love them. If not, I can always melt them down and remake the rings."

"You're not easing my worry, future brother-in-law."

Pearl moved beside him and patted him on the back. "Don't count on becoming his brother. Lillian hasn't accepted a proposal that she hasn't heard yet." Her grin took away any sting the words might have had.

"I guess we'll know that once your husband gets the rings made. I'm planning on proposing at Christmas, so he has to get going on them."

"To that, here are the final drawings." Will handed several sheets of paper to Vernon.

It was just as he had envisioned. Just what he wanted to let the world know how much he loved the woman who he wanted for his wife. He sat in the second swivel chair by the work bench, his heart racing and his breath shallow with awe.

The engagement ring had a heart shaped diamond set in platinum, framed by a lily shape on both sides with smaller round diamonds set in the centers. The petals each had a teardrop diamond.

The wedding ring would encompass the heart with three small diamonds in a fleur-de-lis on the top and rectangular sapphires slanting toward the band. Below, a 'V' of square sapphires would frame the heart, and itself was banded by a decreasing band of diamonds. The rings would nest together once they were married.

"This is just what I hoped it would look like. Thank you."

Will took the drawings and leaned back in his chair. "Vernon, don't think I doubt you and your ability to pay for the rings, but these are going to be very expensive. The gems and platinum alone will cost a lot."

"Don't worry, Will. I have the money to pay for this. When I was young my great-uncle left each of his nieces and nephews legacies with specific instructions on what they were to be used for. It's been in the bank all this time and has grown with the interest.

"Uncle Nate sat me and my brother down. He said that we were only to use the funds to give the woman we married the most magnificent set of rings we could have made. He said that Aunt Penny was the light of his life, and the rings were the first of the many gifts he lavished on her. Those rings were his daily declaration of love for her.

"When we found our loves, we needed to make sure she knew, without a doubt, that, other than the Lord, she was the most important person in our life. That's what I'm doing, making sure Lillian can see my devotion every time she looks at her hand."

"Nate and Penny, where have I heard of them?" Pearl asked. "I know of a couple with those names."

"My grandmother Aggie Cutler was the sister of Nugget Nate Ryder."

"Nugget Nate? The Nugget Nate that all the stories are written about?" Pearl's mouth dropped in shock.

"That be the one. He were jus' a ole mountain man who done jus' what the Lord done tol' him ta do." Vernon imitated his great-uncle's Kentucky mountain accent.

"I read all the stories ever published about him. Do you have Callings like he did? Did your grandmother?" Pearl lowered herself into the chair set at the end of the bench where she crocheted.

"My grandmother always knew when a girl or young lady was in need of help. She always said she collected her girls. She basically rescued them from terrible abusive situations. After my grandfather died, she stayed on the farm until one of the girls she'd helped get away needed her. Mrs. Doc, as we called her, was having twins. So Gramma Aggie moved to Cottonwood, Iowa. She lived there until she passed away."

Vernon laughed. "Aggie always referred to Uncle Nate as Stinky Ryder. There's this hilarious story of when she was little and he got skunked.

"My mother has Callings knowing when babies are going to arrive. She's a midwife. She shows up at the woman's house before they even know they are in labor."

"Do you have Callings?" Pearl was leaning toward him, totally engrossed.

"Yes, to a degree. I can often know what the diagnosis is without even taking any vitals. I don't trust it, since I don't always get the Calling. I also know when something bad is going to happen or has happened to someone I care about."

"That's why you called Lillian that night she burned herself," Will stated.

"Yes, I knew something was wrong with someone. I decided to call everyone I care deeply about. When the operator asked what number, I just knew I should call here."

They were all silent, thinking about Lillian's accident. Finally, Vernon voiced a thought.

"Don't tell Lillian about the Callings and my relationship with Nugget Nate. I'll tell her. It will be better coming from me. I can answer all her questions."

Will and Pearl both nodded as the bell above the shop door jingled and a customer came in. The man strode up to the counter. Will rose to meet him.

"Good afternoon. How may I help you?"

"Where's that sweet little girly who waited on me before?" He leaned over, trying to see if she was in the back room.

The hairs on the back of Vernon's neck rose and his heart tightened. This man meant

Lillian harm. He knew that as well as he knew his name. He knew it was a Calling. Knew the Lord was warning him to keep a close eye on Lillian. To make sure this man never got near her in a way that he could hurt her at all.

"She's not here today. How can I help you?" Will's voice was firm.

"I left my watch to be cleaned a while back. Wondering if it's ready."

"I can check. What's your name?" Will's finger tapped on the glass of the display case.

"Hubbard." The man didn't look or sound pleased to have Will wait on him rather than Lillian.

"Here it is." Will picked a small envelope from a box. He opened it and slid the watch out into his hand. "I cleaned it and adjusted the timing. It should keep better time now."

As Will finished up with Hubbard, Vernon memorized his face and stature. He wanted to be able to recognize him if he ever saw him near Lillian.

CHAPTER THIRTEEN

"Do you remember a customer named Hubbard?" Will asked. "He came in yesterday for his watch." He was wiping the glass cases, but stopped.

Lillian's shoulders gave a shudder. All she wanted to do was forget the man. He gave her the willies. "Yes, did you give it to him?"

"Yes. He asked about you." Will was studying her.

"Oh no. I don't ever want to see him again. He makes me very nervous. He and another man came in together once. They looked around and asked about a few items, then left. I was hoping they wouldn't come back. Hubbard did with his watch, but the other man hasn't. Hubbard came in a couple more times to ask if his watch was done."

"I've never been here when he's come in before."

"He always seems to come in while you are gone for lunch with Pearl or just as I'm closing the shop. Or at least before I moved home. I haven't been here alone in the late afternoon since then."

"Maybe I shouldn't go home for lunch anymore. You fix your lunch here. I could eat here too." Will moved to the next case.

"No, Will. You need time with Pearl before the baby comes. I know she loves having you come home. It also lets her not have to take the trolley when she comes, now that you have your motorcar."

"I don't know. I didn't like the way he looked when he spoke about you."

"I don't like the way he looks period. I hope he never comes back." Lillian nearly stamped her foot, frustrated she couldn't just ban him from the shop.

"Lillian, promise me you'll tell me if he or that other man come in again." Will's tone was full of worry.

"I promise. He gives me the willies, the way he looks at me." Another shudder racked her shoulders

Will set down his rag and came, wrapping his arms around her. Lillian accepted the hug and the comfort her big brother was always able to give her.

~~~~~

Vernon and Lillian took the train to Kansas City to spend Thanksgiving Day with his family. They left on the early morning train and would return that evening. Lillian was both excited and nervous to meet his parents and siblings.

Vernon had told her that his sister, Aggie, was married to a pastor and had three children. His brother, Nathan, had just taken a job with Norfolk Post Card Company. The company had just moved to Kansas City, Missouri from Norfolk, Nebraska and was owned by three brothers by the name of Hall.

Lillian started when Vernon placed his hand over hers. She'd been twisting her lace edged handkerchief that Pearl had given her for her birthday. In her purse were some she was giving to Vernon's mother and sister as a thank you for including her in their holiday. Lillian didn't do lace crochet very well yet, though Pearl was teaching her. She did embroidery well so there were handkerchiefs for his father and brother with their initials stitched on them.

"Don't be nervous. You will charm them without even trying." Vernon gave her hand a squeeze. "There is something I've been wanting to speak to you about."

Lillian's throat tightened. Surely he wasn't going to propose on the train. She knew that was where their relationship was headed. Why ask to court her if he wasn't planning to? But on a train? Not very romantic. Not at all what she'd dreamed of as a little girl. Not at all.

"I've not given you very much background on my family. Since we have time without interruption, I thought this was a good time."

Lillian nearly wiped her hand across her brow in relief. Instead she turned toward him in her seat. "I know about your family. You told me about them, well us really, Pearl was there. It was the first day we met. You stayed for supper with us after Will and my parents left after Father's spell. Your father is Horace, mother is Anna, you have an older sister, Aggie, and younger brother, Nathan. I assume they will all be there today. I'll get to meet them. Is your sister married? Your brother? Their families will be there too, I assume."

Vernon placed his fingers on her lips stopping her flow of words. He chuckled. "You have a very good memory. We've not talked about them since. But that's not what I wanted to talk to you about. It's about my ancestors. One in particular."

"What? Do you have an evil bank robber from the West in your family?"

"No, but maybe just as infamous. My grandmother was born Agatha Ryder. Her brother was Nugget Nate Ryder."

Lillian's mouth dropped open. "No, you're kidding, right? Nugget Nate Ryder?"

"It's true. Hence, my sister's name is Agatha, Aggie, and my brother is Nathan."

"How did you end up as Vernon then?"

"First boy, named after my father's brother." Vernon deadpanned.

"Oh that's right. You mentioned you were named after him and that's why you moved to St. Jo." Lillian leaned back and studied his face. "You don't look like an old mountain man who struck it rich and went around the country catching criminals and rescuing people."

Vernon laughed. "That's because I'm not. He was my great-uncle. I knew him as a very little boy, not long before he died, but I remember him. He and Great-aunt Penny made an impression. They were both unforgettable people. Nate would get going telling a story and Penny would say a word or two and Nate would retell it in a more believable way. I'll have to show you the knife he gave me. It's the very one Jim Bowie gave him after Nate beat him in a fight."

"I read about that in one of the Nugget Nate books. Wow, you must have made an impression on him. You couldn't have been very old when you met him."

Vernon laughed. "I doubt that. Seems that Jim Bowie sent him some crates of the knives. Nate handed them out to lots of boys through the years. Nathan Ryder, The Preacher, found them and a letter after Nate died. Nathan always thought his grandfather was telling each boy a tall tale, but found out he was telling the truth. Those knives had been given to him after that fight."

Lillian was dumbstruck. To have Nugget Nate Ryder and Nathan Ryder, The Preacher, as relatives. That was amazing. "You know The Preacher, too?"

"Yes, he stopped by every time he came through Kansas City. Even came to my sister's wedding, he and Grace."

She bit her lip to keep from asking if they might come to her and Vernon's wedding. He hadn't asked her yet.

"All that is background, really. I had to explain all that to make sure you understand what I'm telling you next. You've read about Nate and his Callings. Well, it runs in the family. Not everyone has them, but many do. It comes from the Ryder side. The stories go way back in the family. My grandmother was a Ryder."

Lillian looked at him, her mind racing. "You have Callings? Like Nugget Nate?"

"Callings, yes. Like Nugget Nate, no. Mine run more in the medical area and concerning people who mean a lot to me. My mother knows when a woman is going into labor. She'll show up at the home just about when the woman begins her labor. She might just up and leave sometime today. We all take it in stride, but I didn't want you to wonder what was going on."

~~~~~

Vernon settled Lillian on the train seat then sat beside her. They were heading back to St. Joseph on the evening train. It would be late when they arrived, but with his motorcar waiting at the station he could have her home shortly after.

"Your family is delightful, Vernon. I had such a good time. I learned a lot about you." She gave him an impish grin.

"I can't believe they told you about the time I fell through the seat in the outhouse. Please don't share that with your family. I think Clyde and Fred, not to mention Will would never let me live it down."

Lillian giggled. "Especially, how you screamed and squealed about all the goo down there."

"Hey, I was only five-years-old."

"And standing on the seat jumping up and down. No wonder the seat broke." Lillian kept giggling, hiding her laughter behind her hand.

Vernon slouched down in mocking disgruntlement. "Not one of my most shining moments."

"No, I suppose not. Don't worry. I won't tell. I wouldn't want my family to think that boy grew up to be a doctor they all respect."

Lillian yawned, hiding it behind her hand. Vernon noticed a tear in a seam of her glove. "Did this happen today?" He took her hand and kissed the finger. "I've never noticed any tears in your gloves before."

"Yes, it tore when I grabbed the handle as I got off the train this morning. I'll sew it up tomorrow. I'm too tired to do it tonight."

Vernon slipped his arm around her. "Lean your head on my shoulder. We were up very early to catch the train. You can doze while we go."

Lillian snuggled close and gave a little sigh. She tucked her hand up under her cheek, ignoring her hat which tipped sideways. Vernon pulled the long hat pin out and tossed the hat onto the seat across from them.

This was so right. His family had loved Lillian, as he'd known they would. Once she got over her shyness, Lillian had blossomed and charmed them as only she could, chattering and laughing along with his family.

Now, all he could do was wait until Christmas. He had his proposal all planned out. He just needed Will to finish the rings.

CHAPTER FOURTEEN

"Lillian's gone for the afternoon. Do you have time to stop in?" It was Will on the telephone. Vernon was hoping it was good news about the rings. Christmas was only a week away.

"Sure, I'll be by around four. I'll come straight from my last house call."

As Vernon left his office, he told the receptionist that he wouldn't return that day. He had a meeting with the other physicians he was hoping to partner with, then several house calls around the city. He worried about how coming into the group would affect his schedule and how Lillian would take it.

Once he was a partner, he'd be on call on a rotating basis for emergency surgeries. There would be times he'd have to remain at home so he could be reached if needed. There would be times he'd get called out in the middle of the night. Lillian wasn't used to anything like that. Her father had always been home at night and available whenever family needed him. This was something he needed to talk with her about before they were married.

Vernon hoped they could be wed soon after Christmas. Well, after they found a house. Maybe that wouldn't take too long. It couldn't be any later than February, surely.

He'd taken the trolley since the streets were somewhat icy. He wasn't confident of his driving around town in these conditions. Vernon looked at his watch as he held the strap. A quarter after four. He wouldn't be too late to get to the shop. He didn't want Will to have to wait on him before he left to go home.

"Come and look, Vernon," Will called as he entered the shop. "They are done. I do believe you will like them."

Vernon held out his hand for the ring box Will held. It was covered in blue velvet. He snapped it open and caught his breath. "Will, I don't know what to say. These are more beautiful than I'd imagined. You can't even tell they are two rings."

"They did turn out well, didn't they? You know, you may have me in the dog house. When Pearl gets a look at these, she's going to want a better ring herself." Will gave him a disgruntle look.

"Hey, you're the cheapskate jeweler who didn't give his wife her due." Vernon couldn't take his eyes off the rings. They were magnificent. He couldn't wait to give them to Lillian. To see the heart shaped diamond on her finger. To add the wedding ring collar. He looked at Will. "You'll keep these for me until Christmas, won't you? If I have them, I'll be sure to propose before the day."

"Of course, I don't want to miss the look on my kid sister's face when she sees these for the first time. Besides, I never turn over a piece of jewelry before it's paid for. It'll stay right in the safe until I see the money."

Vernon set the box on the counter and reached into his jacket pocket. He pulled out his checkbook and pen, paying for the rings with a stroke of his pen.

~~~~~

Her family was acting strange. Yes, it was Christmas and that led to extra excitement in everyone, not just the children. Still, they'd gone to church, then ate Christmas dinner before opening the presents. Vernon had given her a beautiful cashmere shawl in bright red, yellow, and orange flowers. It was beautiful, but not really what she had hoped for.

It was normally the time the small children and men took naps. Instead, everyone was still sitting around the parlor. There was an air of expectancy, but everyone was just chatting. The little ones were running around, excited about not being taken up to bed.

Lillian noticed that Will and Vernon weren't in the room. Oh no, are they cooking up some mischief? Will was known to pull pranks. Was he roping Vernon into it? She wrapped her new shawl around her shoulders and sat in the only open chair. For some reason it was set very near the Christmas tree all by itself.

Will and Vernon came into the room. Will went to stand behind Pearl, laying his hands on her shoulders. Pearl looked up at him and smiled. There was no doubt they were deeply in love. Lillian had known that before they did.

Vernon stood leaning against the mantle. The chatter quieted, and the little ones were placed on laps. Something was up. Were Mary or Josey expecting again? Josey had just had a daughter in October. Surely it had to be Mary. Pearl was days away from giving birth.

Vernon cleared his throat, and everyone looked at him. "I'd like to thank you all for including me in your Christmas celebration. I've felt welcome by you all since I first met you. You've made me feel like family, and I appreciate it." He walked across the room and knelt in front of Lillian.

Lillian's hand went to her mouth. He took her hand.

"Lillian, will you make me truly a part of your family? I love you. Will you marry me?"

She couldn't say a thing. She had no breath. It had all left her lungs when he knelt.

"Look, she's speechless. I didn't think Lillian could ever be speechless," Will said.

His word broke her stupor. Lillian flung her arms around Vernon, knocking him back and they fell on the floor.

"Yes, oh yes. I love you too. I thought you'd never propose."

She scrambled off him and sat up. How embarrassing to be sprawled out on top of a man in front of her family, but Lillian didn't care. Vernon had finally proposed.

He leaned forward and kissed her. "That seals the deal. You can't get out of it now. Your whole family witnessed you accepting, and it was sealed with a kiss."

"You all knew. You all knew he was going to propose. That's why the children aren't down for their naps. That's why you men aren't lying back in chairs snoring," Lillian said as Vernon helped her into her seat. "Well, you all can sure keep a secret better than I can."

Everyone laughed.

"There's one more thing, Lillian," Vernon said and squatted next to her. He held out a velvet covered box and opened it. "Please accept this as a token of my affections. You can only wear one now, but soon, I hope, you'll wear both."

The most beautiful rings she had ever seen sparkled in the light. Lillian's hands began shaking. Never had she thought to wear something this lovely. She picked the rings out of the box.

"Will made these, didn't he?"

"Yes. We designed them together and he created them. May I show you how they link together?" Vernon took the rings and separated them.

"Will, it's beautiful. Thank you." Lillian's eyes were filling with happy tears. Her beloved brother had made rings for her beloved to give to her.

"May I put it on your finger?" Vernon took her left hand in his.

"Oh yes, please do."

As he did so, he whispered for her ears alone. "I love you so very much, my Lillian."

CHAPTER FIFTEEN

Why couldn't the days move faster? Vernon wondered as he drove out of town to make a house call. Why did Lillian want to have a big wedding in June? Why didn't she want to be married in a small ceremony right now?

Pearl's baby had been born at New Years. The little girl, Patricia Luella, was doing well and gaining weight. They were often at the jewelry shop part of each day. Will went to get them and take them home, leaving Lillian to tend the store.

Vernon was now in the physician partnership, which was working out well. Lillian pouted some at his need to be available at all hours some days and nights, but she understood. So she said.

Of course, she'd used it to get him to give her driving lessons during the winter, claiming that if he was going to be limited on leaving the house, she should know how to drive in all conditions. That she thought he'd let her take the motorcar when he might have to hurry to the hospital proved she hadn't thought it through very well. When she did, he was positive she'd be begging him for an automobile of her own. As much in love with her as he was, once he could afford it, he'd most likely purchase her one.

The ladies seemed to like the electric motorcars. They were quiet and easy to start. They also didn't leave smut all over the driver or passengers, so the ladies didn't need to wear goggles and scarves over their faces. One plus to them was that they didn't go very fast or far before needing to be recharged. That would be good for Lillian. It might keep her within the city and not driving at outlandish speeds.

They were nearly settled on the house they wanted to purchase. It wasn't too far from her parents and Will's house. The trolley line was just down the street, so she'd be able to use it to get to work or to family. It wasn't too large or small. They'd be able to start their family before they needed a bigger house.

Starting a family was what he wanted. Or at least doing what was necessary to start a family. Each time he was with Lillian the desire grew stronger. He wished they could marry sooner, but Lillian wanted a June wedding. He'd put his foot down and insisted it be as early in June as possible. June first would be fine with him, but that was a Thursday, so the day he finally made Lillian his wife would be the third.

He'd already made reservations for the honeymoon suite at the Hotel Robidoux for the night. The next day they would leave on the train for Estes Park, Colorado to stay at the new Stanley Hotel for a week.

Between now and then, Lillian planned to keep him busy looking at furniture for the house. It seemed that every Saturday she wanted to spend at least part of the day going to the various furniture stores. They'd decided on the most important piece, at least in his mind. The bed. He really didn't care about any of the other items needed for the house, but she wanted him to be part of choosing each piece.

Lillian had also dragged him all over St. Jo registering them for all sorts of things she said they needed to start housekeeping that they'd receive as gifts. Who would have thought they needed so much stuff? He'd been living quite well with only two place settings of china and silverware. What more did he need? He could get by with one if he made sure to wash them after each meal.

He understood the need for more, since they would be put in the family Sunday afternoon gatherings by fall. Luella had said they'd be exempt until then, being newlyweds and all. Maybe they should purchase a small house like Will and Pearl's. They didn't have to host the family at all. Vernon didn't think Will would be safe from the family for long. Pearl was already hinting they needed a bigger house. There was one for sale only a block from the house he was buying. He'd try to remember to tell Pearl that.

All this wedding planning was eating into his time with Lillian, and that's what bothered him the most. It seemed to be all she wanted to talk about. How her wedding dress was coming along. The house, the wedding showers her sisters and friends were planning. What had happened to the girl who had a million various topics in her head all trying to get out at once? He just hoped she'd come back once the wedding was over, even though it was still months away.

~~~~~

"Drat, I forgot that. I'll need to go over to Townsend and Wyatt's and place that order. We'll need more vases for the flowers at the wedding supper. I can't wait and hope I get some at the showers. I'll have to ask Mother how many Mary and Josey have. I don't want to buy more than we'll need." Lillian was mumbling as she looked over her lists for the wedding.

It was coming so fast. Lillian didn't know how she would get everything done. Well, she'd just pawn some of the chores off on Mary and Josey. She'd certainly done enough for their weddings.

Maybe she shouldn't have insisted on making her wedding gown, at least the underdress. Pearl was making a lace dress just as she had for Daisy Clary. At least the silk was here.

Lillian had ordered it as soon as she could get to Townsend and Wyatt after Christmas. She'd gone straight to Mr. Dimmick and asked him to place her order. Then she'd given him a quick peck on the cheek and told him she would be sure not to drop it.

Setting the lists down, Lillian held up her left hand. The diamond ring sparkled. She couldn't wait until the sapphires and diamonds of the wedding ring surrounded the heart. Maybe she shouldn't have insisted on a June wedding. No, there was no way she would be ready before then. Her mother was helping, but the lists seemed to keep getting longer.

The shop door opened with a jingle of the bell attached. Lillian looked to see who was coming in. Her stomach dropped. The two men who'd been coming in and bothering her ran around the counter. Lillian stood and began to run up the stairs to lock herself in the apartment. One of the men tackled her as she got to the fifth step.

"Come on, girly. You're going with us." He hauled her up and pinned her against the wall. "You're gonna walk out of here quietly, or I'll just bash you on the head and carry you out." He had bushy brown eyebrows.

"How are you going to get me to keep quiet while you take me down the street? People will see me and know I wouldn't ever go with you."

"Not a problem." The other man brought her coat and hat. His ears stuck straight out from his head. "Put this on." He tossed her coat to her. Bushybrows let her go but kept her from going up the stairs. Ears stood at the bottom so she couldn't escape that way.

"Why are you doing this? I'll give you jewelry. Just leave me here." Lillian put her coat on with shaking fingers.

"Too hard to fence. We wouldn't get enough for them, but your folks will pay top dollar to get you back. That man you've been seeing will too. Figure we'll send ransom notes to both. Get double that way."

She finally got her coat buttoned. How could she get away? She couldn't believe they were kidnapping her in the middle of the day. Sure, the day was overcast so it was darker than normal. It was also cold and windy, typical March weather. Few customers had ventured out. Will had gone home for lunch. She glanced at the clock. He wouldn't be back for at least a half hour.

How to let him know she didn't leave willingly? Ears plopped her hat on and secured it with a veil wrapped to obscure her face. Anyone out on the street wouldn't realize it was her.

"Come on. Let's go."

As they moved past the bench, Lillian began to struggle. She knew she'd never escape. That wasn't her intent. She wrenched her arm out of Bushybrow's grasp and kicked out at him. He jumped back, but came at her quickly. Between the two of them, her lists, jeweler's loops, and tool fell to the floor.

Ears jerked her to him. "Stop that or I'll beat you senseless."

Lillian stilled. She'd accomplished what she wanted. Will would never believe she'd leave with all that scattered on the floor. She just hoped the men wouldn't notice.

"Come on. Let's get out of here." Bushybrows grabbed her other arm and pulled her along with them.

The question of how they would get away from the shop with her in tow was answered when they stepped outside. A delivery truck was parked but running at the curb.

Ears let go of her arm, opened the door and shoved her in. Bushybrows ran around to the driver's side and got in before she could scramble to the other side of the seat. Now, she was stuck between them.

"See girly, it wasn't so hard to get you away from the shop with no one the wiser." Ears patted her thigh as they drove out of town.

~~~~~

"Answer the telephone, please, answer the telephone," Vernon begged. All morning the feeling in his stomach that he knew was a Calling had grown. He'd been assisting in surgery all morning. The last one was finally finished. He'd stitched the man closed and hurried out of the operating room. His partner was telling the family of the operation's success. Vernon had gone straight to the telephone and called the jewelry shop. Either Lillian or Will would be there. Should be there.

"I'm sorry, sir," the operator said, "no one seems to be answering. Please try your call later." The connection clicked out.

Vernon leaned against the wall. Something had happened to Lillian. He knew it. The Calling was too strong to be anything else. Standing straight, he rang the operator again and gave her Will's number.

"Hello?" Pearl answered.

"Pearl, is Will with you and Lillian?" Please be there. Please be there.

"No, Vernon, Will just left. Lillian stayed at the shop while he came home for lunch. Is something wrong?"

"I tried calling the shop and there's no answer. I'm having a Calling and I'm sure it's about Lillian. I need to know if she's all right."

"Oh dear. Will should be there in a few minutes. How can he get ahold of you? Are you at your office?" Pearl sounded worried. Vernon certainly was.

"I'm at the hospital. I'm going to the shop. I need to talk with Will. Pray, Pearl, please. This is the strongest Calling I've ever had. Something terrible has happened to her, I just know."

"I will. You go now." Pearl hung up on him.

Vernon ran down the hall, pulling his surgery coat off. "I'm going to be gone the rest of the day. An emergency. Let my office know," he said as he ran past the admitting desk.

Vernon ran down the street. A light mist filled the air, whipped by the wind. He burst into the shop, jumping the steps without touching them.

"Is Lillian here?" He saw Will looking down at the floor by the workbench. He rounded the counter, trying to catch his breath.

"No. The door was unlocked and there's stuff scattered all over back here," Will said.

"Something's happened to her. I've been getting a Calling all morning. I couldn't come because I was in surgery. It started small but kept growing. In the last little while it's gotten so much stronger. I couldn't keep from coming."

"You've not told us much about the Callings. Is there a way you can know where she is and what's happened to her?" Will grabbed Vernon's arm.

Vernon took a deep breath. "I've never had one this strong before, not even when Lillian burned herself. I just knew it was about her."

"Now what? How good is it when we don't know where she is?"

Suddenly, Vernon knew what he needed to do. Nugget Nate had told him, when he was little, and Nathan Ryder had later, that he needed to listen to the Calling. It would direct him where he should go. When he got there, he'd know what was needed.

"Is your motorcar here, Will?"

"No, since Pearl isn't coming in today, I rode the trolley."

"Then I'll have to go back to the hospital. Mine's there."

"You aren't going without me. You'll need to get your coat too. You ran here without it. No use catching pneumonia."

Will shrugged on his coat and locked the door as they left. Vernon took off at a run, his Calling urging him to hurry.

It wasn't long before they were in the vehicle, Vernon driving, following the turns his Calling told him to use.

~~~~~

These sure were stupid kidnappers. They didn't even tie me up. If they weren't on both sides of me, I could just jump out and run. They'd probably catch me though.

Lillian sat between Bushybrows and Ears. The truck was stolen from where they worked, delivering supplies between warehouses and factories. They'd told her to just shut up when she began to talk their ears off. That the words had been accompanied by a slap to her face made her obey. Now, she was watching the road. Boy, were these kidnappers stupid.

Lillian knew this road. She'd driven it often for her driving lessons. It wasn't too well travelled, so that was a smart choice for them, but she knew all about it. She also knew where to turn to get to another road that would lead back to St. Joseph. All she had to do was wait.

It wasn't long. Lillian looked down to keep her grin from alerting them that they were about to lose control of the situation. Yes, she knew this road and what lay just around the curve.

Slurch. The truck hit the mud where a small stream sometimes crossed the dirt road.

And stopped. Bushybrows pulled the accelerator handle toward him, and the wheels spun, throwing mud up behind them.

"Get this thing moving," Ears shouted. Lillian covered her ears with her hands. Bushybrows yelled back that he was trying.

She let them argue for several minutes. They tried different speeds attempting to get the truck moving. Finally, they stopped and Bushybrows said, "You're going to have to get out and push."

"Why me?" Ears said.

"'Cause I'm driving, idiot."

Ears turned to Lillian. "You're gonna stay right here. You run and you'll regret it when I catch you, and I will."

"Yes, sir," Lillian said meekly.

Ears got out and went behind the truck. "Okay, I'm pushing."

Bushybrows pulled the accelerator handle down again. The wheels spun and Ears screamed.

"Stop. You're spraying me with mud." He stomped back to look in the window by Lillian. "This thing is too big for one man to push. You'll have to come help. All that tire spinning has sunk it deeper."

"I can't do that. Someone has to drive." Bushybrows smacked the steering wheel.

"Well, unless you want to stay here until the road dries, you're going to have to help me push. She can hold the wheel straight surely. Just make sure it's in low gear and show her how to make it go."

Bushybrows pursed his lips. He was obviously trying to think of some other way to do it. Lillian didn't say a thing. She just waited until they told her what to do. Then she'd do as told until the truck was out of the mud.

"You, girly. Look here. You're gonna sit here and not touch anything but the wheel and this here lever. When I tell you, pull it to here. Only to here, no further. Got it?"

"Yes, sir." Lillian scooted behind the wheel as Bushybrows got out.

"Remember, just the wheel and the lever."

She nodded.

They walked to the back of the truck. "Okay, pull the lever."

Lillian pulled, maybe a little further than Bushybrows had told her. Mud splattered and the tires spun. Then the truck began to move and the men pushed.

As soon as the truck was out of the mud, Lillian pulled the lever lower, released the clutch while she pushed the brake handle all the way forward. The truck sped down the road with two mud covered men yelling for her to stop as they ran behind.

~~~~~

"How do you know we're on the right road?" Will asked.

Vernon shook his head. "It's the Calling. It's telling me which way to go. The Calling is from God so I know it's right. If I follow the Calling, we'll find her."

They'd travelled out of town and were on a road Vernon had taken Lillian on several times. They usually came home this way when they'd had a driving lesson.

"Keep a look out for Lillian. I know we'll find her along this road somewhere."

They ignored the truck coming toward them until it stopped and the door opened. Then, Vernon halted his motorcar and jumped out.

Lillian had exited the truck and was running toward him. Vernon scooped her up in his arms, kissing her until Will cleared his throat.

"Vernon, I was so scared. They came into the shop and grabbed me. I struggled to knock things off the bench. I knew Will would know something was wrong. They put me between them in the truck. They stole the truck from their work. They were going to send ransom notes to both you and Father. They took the same road we always had driving lessons on. The truck got stuck, and they pushed while I drove. I left them covered in mud, yelling at me to stop. I didn't, of course. Then I just drove away. I knew where to turn to get onto this road. I was going back to town. I'm so glad you found me. We need to contact the police."

Vernon just kept holding her. He couldn't say anything, his relief that she was okay made words impossible.

"Hi, Will." Lillian kept her arms around him so tightly he could barely breath. That was just fine with him.

"Hi, Lill. I'm so glad you escaped." He kissed her cheek. "Now, we need to get back to town and take this truck to the police. I'll drive it. You go with Vernon. I don't think he'll want you out of his sight until he leaves you in Father's arms."

"You are right about that," Vernon said and loosened his hold on Lillian. "Let's go."

Lillian stayed tucked against him just where he wanted her.

"Can I drive?"

Vernon threw his head back and laughed. Will joined in as he climbed into the truck.

"Yes, my dear, you may drive."

CHAPTER SIXTEEN

Lillian stood at the back of the church in her silk and lace gown. Her hand was tucked into her father's elbow. The bridesmaids were walking up the aisle. Soon she would become Mrs. Vernon Strasser.

"Well, my dear, it's time. Your mother and I love you very much. We loved raising you, but you're a beautiful woman in all ways. You've found a wonderful young man." He kissed her cheek. A teasing twinkle appeared in his eyes. "You've driven us crazy many times over the years. Now, I'm sure, you will be driving Vernon crazy."

"Oh, Papa." Lillian used the name she'd called him until she was a teen.

The music changed and they walked down the aisle. She only had eyes for Vernon. The minister began the familiar words, but she didn't hear any until he asked who gave her away. Then her father placed her hand in Vernon's, and they ascended the steps for their vows.

Her hand was trembling when Vernon said, "With this ring I thee wed, and all my earthly goods I thee endow."

The rings were now nestled together and slipped onto her finger.

At last, the minister said the words she was longing to hear. "I now pronounce you man and wife. You may kiss your bride."

Vernon did.

~~~~~

"I can't believe they did that to your motorcar." Lillian covered her ears as the clatter and bang of tin cans tied to the back fender bounced on the pavement.

"It's all in good fun. It lets everyone know you are mine now." Vernon didn't care about the noise. Lillian was his wife. They were driving to the reception which was being held in the ballroom of the Robidoux. He hoped they could get away from the celebration early. He had other plans for the evening than being with friends and family.

They pulled up in front of the hotel. Vernon turned to Lillian and whispered, "Let's escape to our room as early as we can."

A gleam came into her eyes. She smiled wide. "Okay, but only if I can drive to the train station tomorrow."

A Note From Sophie

I hope you enjoyed **Driving Lillian**. Please take a moment to leave a review on Amazon. For independently publishing authors like myself, the reviews are extremely valuable in getting our work noticed. If you take just a few minutes you could help someone else find their next favorite book.

You can post a review right from your Kindle or Kindle app. Just scroll past the end of the book. The form will pop up. Although Amazon says they require 20 words they will post it with fewer. You can pad your review with the title of the book and author name.

If you've missed any of my books or want to read more of them, head to my Amazon Author page. http://amazon.com/author/sophiedawson

Here are ways you can keep up with my sales and upcoming releases.

Sign up for my newsletter.

https://mailchi.mp/449be73f3465/sophiedawsonnewsletter

Join my Sophie's Reader Friends group on Facebook.

https://www.facebook.com/groups/139425236751751/

Thank you.

Sophie